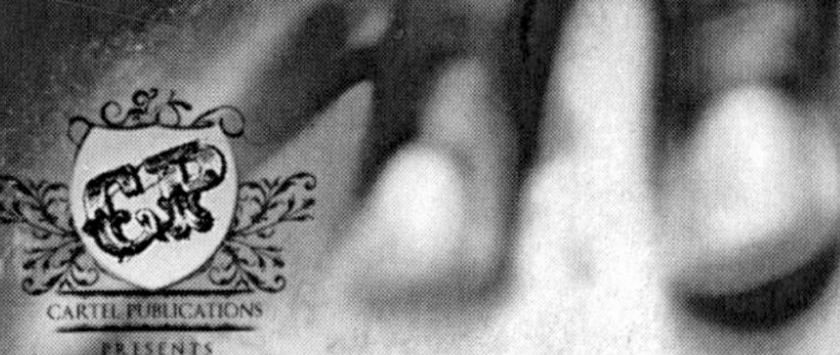

THEIR DESIRE TO GET HIGH WILL COST THEM MORE THAN THEIR LIVES

DEAD HEADS

a chilling novel

VJ GOTASTORY

AUTHOR OF *YEAR OF THE CRACKMOM*

PUBLISHER'S NOTE:
This book is a work of fiction. Names, characters, businesses, Organizations, places, events and incidents are the product of the Author's imagination or are used fictionally. Any resemblance of Actual persons, living or dead, events, or locales are entirely coincidental.

Library of Congress Control Number: 2012930044
ISBN 10: 0984993029
ISBN 13: 9780984993024
Cover Design: Davida Baldwin www.oddballdsgn.com
Editor: Advanced Editorial Services
Graphics: Davida Baldwin
www.thecartelpublications.com
First Edition

Printed in the United States of America

CHECK OUT OTHER TITLES BY THE CARTEL PUBLICATIONS

Shyt List 1
Shyt List 2
Shyt List 3
SHYT LIST 4
Shyt List 5
Pitbulls in a Skirt 1
Pitbulls in a Skirt 2
Pitbulls In A SKirt 3
Poison 1
Poison 2
Victoria's Secret
Hell Razor Honeys 1
Hell Razor honeys 2
Black and Ugly As Ever
A Hustler's Son 2
The Face That Launched A Thousand Bullets
Year of the Crackmom
The Unusual Suspects
Miss Wayne and the Queens of DC
La Familia Divided
Raunchy
Raunchy 2: Mad's Love
Reversed
Quita's DayScare Center
Dead Heads
The End. How To Write A Bestselling Novel in 30 Days

WWW.THECARTELPUBLICATIONS.COM

ACKNOWLEDGEMENTS

GOD First!

My deepest and sincere thanks to every one of the loyal readers who faithfully support the Cartel Publications. Thank you as well for your support of my first book entitled, "Year of the Crack Mom". I could not have written it without the help of famed author, T. Styles. She deserves all the credit. Thank you Ms. Styles.

To my beloved brothers and sisters: Tony (Butch) – Marvene (Veenie) – Florence (Dani) and Quentin. You are the other halves of my life. I love you dearly.

To my Mom (Aundrea) and Daddy Harold and my mother in-law- Mom (Brenda). I love you so much!

To my beloved cousins: Rev Thad-Louis and Tracy, Thelma, . Eric, Twain, Ivy, Traci-Lynn, and Sharmaine. You are the cousins with whom I have shared my life with. I love you all.

My one and only son; my love for you goes beyond what words can describe. You are the joy of my life. I love you more than life itself.

To my select few: Mona Taylor, Robin Frisby, Corey Young, Charles Newah, Willis Gamory, Sofia Liarakos, Brian Barrett and Carolyn Victorian. Your friendships are priceless and I value each and every one of them. I love you all.

To my Facebook friends, thank you for your continued support of the Cartel Publications and VJ Gotastory!

And God Always Gets the Glory!

DEDICATION

GOD First!

This book is dedicated to the following:

Edwin, my wonderful loving husband; your recent fight and survival of Cancer, coupled with your Sickle Cell disease have taught me many things. Most of all your survival taught me how to survive, how to be patient, how to love deeper and to cherish life as never before and most of all to trust in GOD. I love you with everything in me and from the bottom of my heart.

My beautiful-wonderful granddaughters; Kaviah, Taylor, Diearra and Brittany. My handsome-wonderful nephew, Gaston. My beautiful-wonderful niece Toni. I love you all. You make my world such a happier place. There is nothing like wrapping my arms around my babies and squeezing all of my love and happiness on you when I see you.

What's Good Babies,

I hope everything you desire is popping up in your world along with a few great things you didn't imagine. For me, well, at the time this novel was published, I was in need of some mental healing. Although a lot of positive things are happening in my world, good stress is still stress and should be dealt with. So I took a much-needed retreat and begin my search for positive ways to improve my mind. What I found was something called the Gerson Therapy. Although the Gerson Therapy is geared toward people who have cancer, I felt if I followed the regimen, that it could do wonders for my mind. I was correct. Since then I've experienced clarity like I never have, and a rejuvenated spirit. I call out to anyone afflicted with any debilitating disease, to read up on this therapy, which is outlawed in the United States, despite its wondrous results.

Now, once your mind is right, hopefully we can twist it up again with V.J's newest novel, *DeadHeads.* I absolutely love books with refreshing concepts and ideas, and V.J, did not disappoint with her mind altering latest novel. So sit back, relax and read away.

Before you go, keeping in line with Cartel tradition, where we honor an author who we admire on his journey, I would like to pay tribute to the late:

Dr. Max Gers□n, M.D.

As mentioned in my letter, his book titled, *The Gerson Therapy,* has done wondrous things for people afflicted by illnesses from cancer to the common cold. I pray that the book finds you in good hands for all those who need the message.

Until we speak again,

T. Styles, President & CEO
The Cartel Publications
www.thecartelpublications.com
www.facebook.com/authortstyles
www.twitter.com/authortstyles

CHEMISTRY 101

The dim light radiated from the broken light fixture overhead, and cast a shadow on the G4-22 Glock as it sat proudly in the middle of the warped lopsided table. The table was surrounded by three in debtors. Included in the three was Bonita, a once beautiful, thick bodied, bronze skinned dime. Every man young and old wanted to tag that ass. When Bonita walked down the street, she stopped all games of dominoes, spades, chess and rambunctious games of craps. Every man's dick swelled in his pants as she walked by. Her ass was the phattest ass ever seen on a small-framed woman. Her smile could melt the coldest man's heart and she was always rockin' the latest clothing, shoes and bags. But today, Bonita sat at the table zoned out.

She was skinny and almost bald. She no longer had an interest in her looks so she cut her hair off to keep from having to deal with it on a daily basis. The musty and sour smell that came from under her arms and between her thighs was a result of her ass not being near water for more than a week. You could smell her foulness up, over, around and across the table. The radiant smile that once lit up a room when she entered was no longer there. Several teeth were missing from her mouth. Now she was called snaggled-tooth Deadhead behind her back by her neighbors and the local drug dealers. Bonita didn't give a damn as she anxiously a waited her turn.

Everyone at the table was a slave to this new highly submissive, mind altering, zombiefing mix. The drug's creator was Stic whose real name is Sticory. Stic was a bookworm with a lot of book smarts. He always had a nerdy kinda mixed up side to him and people were often misled by that nerdy mixed up shit. But if one really looked into Stic's eyes they would see a demonic spirit lived within his soul. While in high school, Stic befriended a stringy, oily haired white boy name Aston. Aston was fascinated with making concoctions that could be induced for getting high and often he and Stic would work in Aston's garage lab inventing shit. Stic never fucked with using any of the wild shit that Aston made but Aston on the other hand coaxed his friends into being the guinea pigs for his inventions. More often than enough, his friends, and Aston himself, ended up adversely ill or they stayed high for hours on end. After seeing how easy it was to mix some shit up, Stic thought wisely and devised a plan to use his mind to make him millions. Stic wanted the grand life and he was determined to do something no one else could do or copy.

After a long talk with Aston, Stic decided he was going straight to college after high school. He made the announcement to his mother who was beside herself with joy. She worked three jobs to provide some of the money he would need for school. It was a long and heavy sacrifice on her behalf, but his mother was determined to see her baby graduate. She was so proud of him. Stic however, had ulterior motives for going to college. He had it mapped out and kept in constant contact with Aston. Once Sticory graduated with a degree in biochemistry and pharmacology from the University of Baltimore, he looked up his old friend Aston and they had a meeting. With his vast knowledge of chemistry and pharmacology, both he and Aston, worked in a lab for months and created a new drug that could not be duplicated. This was not crack or meth, naw this shit was much harder. It was more powerful than both and its addictive state was almost 100% after the first hit. He had several guinea pigs who could vouch for that, if they ever stopped smoking long enough to think on their own. Because the drug was almost hypnotic in its affects, Stic gave it the name *Mind Bend*. The ingredients would remain a secret only shared by Stic and Aston.

The only written copy of the drug was on an encrypted flash drive, that was stored in a safety deposit box in a bank in another state. Aston didn't know this and didn't know that his name was all over the document either. In case some shit happened, the white boy could not wiggle his ass out of trouble and leave Stic holding the bag. Fuck that shit! If Stic went down, the white boy went down too. And what Stic didn't know is that Aston had everything they said and did on an encrypted flash drive himself. Shit, that white boy was no fool. He knew Stic would roll over his ass at the drop of a dime. He also knew Stic was cold and calculating and very dangerous. Aston stayed clear not to cross Stic or get on his bad side. Those that did were dealt with severely and or never heard from again. Aston gave his flash drive to his sister for safekeeping. If anything happened to Aston, Stic's ass was going down…way down. Stic worked with one of the most notorious crime families in the Baltimore area in a laundry money scam, as well as fencing gold and diamonds for several wealthy Africans. Stic had many irons in many fires that produced many avenues of income, but he loved only two of those avenues. "Mind Bend" and "Get it Up" productions, which Stic produced movies under.

However, today Stic was talking to Aston about some type of chip that could be planted in a person's body and that person would just about do whatever you wanted them to do. Aston wasn't sure about this concept but knowing Stic, he did his homework and if it could be done, then Aston could bet his skinny white cracker ass Stic was already on it. Aston knew it was just a matter of time before Stic would have a vested interest in the imbedded chip theory. Stic was at one of his secret hideaways that only a few people were allowed to come to. You only came to the spot to get high or pick up product. If you came to get high, you were practically blindfolded and lead into another room. This location was also used as a final destination for those whose number was up according to Stic. Stic had this, and one other location, specifically outfitted for murder. Clean up was a breeze because his crazy ass had everything made out of recycled plastic from the walls, to the ceiling and floor. The entire room was soundproofed.

Stic sat on his throne and watched the deadheads continue to get high. He loved this shit. He was in control and could do whatever the fuck he wanted to do to them. He named them Deadheads because after smoking Mind Bend they're brains were dead. They acted on command or impulse. Stic knew the trio at the table personally, which was an added bonus. Stic stood up from his throne. Yeah…the nigga actually had a gold throne done in an exact replica of one he once saw on the history channel during an episode on the "Kings of Egypt". Stic's throne was carved of wood and then the armchair was covered with more than fifty thousand dollars worth of pure gold. Stic methodically walked around the room observing the activity within it. The Deadheads at the table were zoned out but were aware of his presence. He stopped midway through his walk and addressed the table.

"You, Deadheads have had enough freebies. I need some money. Show me the fuckin' money!" One of Stic's soldiers snatched the tray, that held the beloved drug, off the table. All three of the Deadheads immediately started to fidget in their chairs. No one said a word or went into their pockets for the money that Stic requested. Secretly, Stic smiled within because he knew none of them could pay for their hits. He owned them. He could play his games now. He continued to walk around the table and talk.

"I'm gonna ask you motherfucka's again, where's the money?"

Several more seconds of silence was interrupted by Dawn, a red, pimple faced white girl sitting to the right of Bonita. "I don't have no more money, Stic. I just gave you my last." She whined.

"Is that so? Stic smirked. His constant walking around and behind the Deadheads was making them all nervous as shit. The wonderful high that they were experiencing was now being replaced with agitation and fear. Stic abruptly stopped and pointed his finger across the table. "What about you, nigga, you got any money?" Stic asked Whizzie.

Wide eyed and shaking in his drawers, Whizzie couldn't answer. Whizzie was a fat, blacker than tar and always wheezing short man. He had the worst asthma and used his asthma as an excuse to keep the social security checks rolling in so his ass didn't have to go to work. Now, he was sitting up at the table wheezing his way to a high. He looked and sounded pathetic as he found his voice and spoke.

"Naw, Stic, I spent all my ends with you, too. I ain't got shit right now!" Whizzie said eyeing the Glock that was still lying in the middle of the table. He wondered what it would be like to snatch the gun off the table and shoot Stic in the throat. But Whizzie knew of Stic's reputation, it preceded him. He also knew his chances of that happening and not being killed on the spot was like his fat ass saying no, to a free all you can eat buffet.

"Ummm hmmmm, so don't none of ya'll got no money!? Is that what the fuck ya'll sayin'? So ya'll just sat your asses around my table like knights and smoked up a crypt of Mind Bend? I know damn well ya'll don't think I'm just gonna let your asses leave up outta here without some form of payment right?" He said eyeing each one of them.

Bonita spoke next. "We paid you for our packages and then you put another crypt down on the table. You didn't say nothing about we had to pay for it. Come on, Stic, you set us up."

"Set you up? Bitch, didn't nobody set ya'll asses up. All ya'll sat down at this table and took part in the smoke fest. And you bitches had ample opportunity to get the fuck up and leave. Especially when you knew your motherfuckin' pockets had holes in 'em. You motherfucka's set yourselves the fuck up!" Stic continued with his tirade.

Bonita pushed her chair away from the table and Stic immediately slammed that ass back down into her seat with such a force, her chair toppled over onto the white girl. Bonita recovered with embarrassment as she stared up at Stic. He was laughing at her. He pointed to each person at the table, the white girl, the short wheezing man and Bonita. "I'ma need something from each of you motherfucka's for payment. Ya'll betta think." Stic said singing the statement in the tune of Aretha Franklin's song *'You Better Think'*.

"Tick tock, tick tock, tick tock," Stic said mocking the sound of a clock. After several minutes of silence, Stic's impatience grew. He nodded his head to Skibop, his right hand solider. Skibop approached the table and snatched the G4-22 Glock off it and handed the Glock to Stic. Skipbop opened the door to let in extra backup. Incoming was Batman and Moop, two more of Stic's boys. They posted up around the table. Stic took the glock and slipped in a magazine. He pulled back the slide, which injected a bullet into the chamber. All eyes were on him. Whizzie felt stupid when he saw Stic put the clip in the gun. He couldn't believe that he thought about snatching it and trying to shoot his way out and the motherfucker didn't have nare bullet inside.

He imagined his fat ass stretched out on the floor dead as hell. He shook his head at his own stupidness.

The white girl decided it was her turn to speak. "What are you going to do?" Dawn stammered. Stic didn't reply as he continued to load the Glock.

Whizzie suddenly had another brilliant bright ass idea; he decided he was just going to get the hell up from the table. That most definitely proved to be the wrong fucking move for the asthmatic man. Skibop immediately reacted to the bold move and delivered a blow to the fat man's face sending him over the side of the table and down onto the floor. Several heavy quick stomps to his face ensured a broken nose. Bonita and Dawn were screaming like banshees. Skibop continued his stomp fest on the man as guns were drawn from the other soldiers who stood guard around the table.

"Shut the fuck up or all ya'll will be bodied!" One of the soldiers shouted. He waved his tactical semi automatic at the girls and suddenly their screams became childlike whimpers. Skibop finished his ass whooping on Whizzie and then pulled Whizzie's bloody heap of mass up off the floor and threw him back into a chair. Whizzie was semi-conscious. His head rolled from side to side as slobber, snot and blood ran freely from his mouth, nose and head. Stic walked behind the fat man and slapped him upside his head with the butt of his glock. "Simple motherfucka!" he mumbled. Bonita and Dawn watched Stic with frightful eyes. Stic sat down on the side of the table and looked at each girl. He sucked his teeth with disdain as he eyeballed them. He casually placed the gun down at his side. He sniffed hard and looked at his newly manicured hands.

"Okay, seeing that we've got to the end of the road," he burst out laughing and continued on, "Let's play a game. You know that song that Rihanna sings called, *'Russian Roulette'*? Well we're about to see if you know the true meaning of it." Dawn slowly stood up and stumbled towards Stic. All the gunmen immediately aimed their weapons of choice at her. Stic raised his hand and the gunmen slightly lowered their arsenal. Stic wanted to see how far Dawn would go to plead for her life. She tried to be sexy as she sauntered up to Stic and placed her pasty white skinny hand on his crotch.

She cocked her head to the side and said, "Let me take care of you, Stic. You know I can do it good. Let me just show you." She said trying to unzip Stic's pants. He scrunched up his face and pushed her away from him.

"Crazy nasty ass, white bitch! You ain't got nothing I fuckin' want. Not even some Becky. Sit your dumb ass back down in that chair and don't say shit else!"

Dawn wasn't giving up that easily. "Come on, Stic, let me show you what I can do." Stic raised his hand and slapped Dawn so hard across her face that she twirled around like a ballerina and fell to the floor. She immediately screamed obscenities at Stic as she lay there holding her face.

"Set that wack ass bitch back up and let's play!" he yelled. Moop snatched Dawn up and put her back in her chair. "You got anything to say?" Stic asked looking coldly at Bonita. Bonita looked over at Whizzie who was a battered mess and was now out cold. She then looked at Dawn's tear streaked, swollen face and slowly shook her head no. "Good, that's what the fuck I thought. Now let the game begin." Stic turned on his Nikes and walked back to his throne. "Since you three motherfucka's can't pay the required amount of thirty dollars each, for your share of the party favors, I'ma have to shut this party down with a game that I've always wanted to play but never had the balls to play myself. Now, I have just the right amount of players and today is your lucky fuckin' day. Batman, spin the six!" Batman reached behind his back and pulled out a Colt six-shooter and placed it on the table.

Batman grinned hard at Bonita and Dawn and said, "I've seen this game played before and nobody ever fucking wins. Good luck." He snickered and stepped back.

Stic intervened, "The rules of the game are simple. Pick up the gun, open the cylinder, spin the barrel and snap it shut. When you do that, place that shit up to your head and pull the trigger. You two bitches got it?" He crossed his legs and sat back further into his throne. Bonita turned to Stic with pleading eyes.

"Stic, you ain't serious about this is you? We only owe you thirty dollars. Why can't you let me and Dawn work out something with you and your crew? I'll do whatever you want, Stic. Please don't make us play this game. I've got a daughter. She needs me, Stic. Who's gonna raise my child?"

"Perhaps you should have thought about that when you was coming up in here getting your high on. Did you forget, Bonita that you already indebted to me? I let your ugly ass slide last time; I'm not about to let it go this time. Now you and snow white there are going to play this game or I'ma send Batman over there with his bat to concave both of your skulls in. Now pick the gun up and let's fuckin' play." Batman and Moop raised their guns and aimed them at Dawn and Bonita. Neither one wanted to go first so Stic sensing their hesitation reached into his pocket and pulled out a quarter.

"Bonita, call it." He said as he flipped the quarter in the air. Bonita didn't say a word. She watched the coin leave Stic's hand, glide through the air and land back into the palm of his hand. "You ain't call nothing, Bonita! Fuck it then, I'll call it. How about heads!" He opened his hand and the quarter revealed the spread eagle. Bonita let out a sigh of relief. Dawn was not so lucky. Moop pushed the barrel of his gun in the back of Dawn's head.

"Pick that shit up." He said. Dawn began to cry. "You can either play the game or I will simply eliminate you as a willing participant." Moop said. Dawn's hand slowly moved towards the

Colt. Shaking, she picked it up and felt the weight in her grasp. She pulled the gun towards her.

"Go on, stop fuckin' playin'! I got shit to do!" Moop said as he mushed the back of Dawn's head again with the barrel of his semi automatic. She hesitated again and Moop released the safety on his weapon. With no way out, Dawn released the cylinder, spun the chamber, shut it back and put it to her head while pulling the trigger. Bonita jumped up screaming as brain matter and blood splattered her face and clothes. Bonita fell over backwards in the chair as she frantically brushed her face and arms free of the bloody debris.

"Now that was fucking impressive! One roll of the chamber and pa-dow, just like that one player is eliminated! Get up, Bonita, your turn, baby girl!" Stic said feeling his dick get hard from the excitement of death. Moop snatched a still screaming Bonita by her arms and set her up right in her chair. "Shut that bitch up right now!" Stic continued. Moop stuck his gun under Bonita's chin.

"You heard the man. Shut the fuck up or the only player left will be fat boy over there, he said nodding towards a now conscience Whizzie. Bonita's screams turned into pleading sentences for her life. She sat in the chair next to a slumped over Dawn who was dead and had fallen onto the table, eyes wide open, mouth agape with a self inflicted bullet to the right side of her head. Blood fanned out across the table like water that spilled from a glass. Half of the top of Dawn's head was blown around the room. Bonita willed herself not to vomit. She scooted her blood-splattered chair away from the corpse. Moop pushed the gun into Bonita's hand.

"Stic, please…Please don't make me do this! Please…My daughter needs me Stic, I'll do anything!" Bonita said between deep sobs. She put the gun down and fell out the chair on her knees. With hands folded in a prayer fashion she walked on her knees towards Stic pleading for her life. Stic watched in amusement at Bonita's desperate act. He waited until she was in front of his throne when he took his right foot and kicked her over. She fell sideways but that didn't deter her from knee walking back to Stic.

"I'm begging for my life. Please, Stic!" she sobbed. Stic stood up and looked down at the broken woman that was on bended knees in front of him. He walked around her in a circle and stopped behind her. He knelt down behind her and whispered in her ear.

"How is that pretty daughter of yours?" Bonita didn't answer. Stic grabbed her by the back of her neck and turned her face to his. "Again", he whispered in her ear, "how is your daughter?"

"She's fine. Why?" Bonita stammered.

"She's practically grown ain't she, so she really don't need you to raise her anymore." Stic said.

"Cherry is my child, Stic. She still needs me, I'm her mother. All children need their mothers." Bonita uttered.

Stic pulled Bonita closer and said, "Okay, Bonita, I got one more game to play. It's called, *Let's Make a Deal*. Here's the deal. Your life for Cherry's."

"What do you mean my life for Cherry's? Are you going to kill my child instead of me?" Bonita whispered.

"No, I'm not going to body her. I don't hurt nothing that belongs to me." Bonita vigorously shook her head no. "Bonita, the stakes have just gotten higher now. You can either give Cherry to me and live, or you can choose not to and I kill Cherry any damn way just because you're making this decision to damn hard. If you choose to play the Roulette game like your dead friend did, then, I'ma let that fat wheezing motherfucker put the gun up to your head and pull the trigger. And if his ass doesn't choose to participate," Stic threw a look towards Whizzie, "then you will kill him." Stic said pointing at Whizzie, "And then I'ma let Batman do his thang on you with his bat. He ain't had no runs batted lately." Stic laughed. He abruptly stopped and turned his attention back to Bonita. He peered down in her terrified face and snarled, "Either way, Bonita you lose. So why don't we make a deal." Bonita hung her head and cried. Stic looked down at her with contempt. He sucked his teeth and nodded his head towards Batman.

"Please don't, Stic."

"Clean up this shit. All of it! And make sure she understands that Cherry is mine! And I don't give a shit what you do with fat boy over there! It's your motherfuckin' party, Batman!" Stic and Moop walked out the door leaving Batman, Whizzie and Bonita behind.

Bonita immediately tried to appeal to Batman. "Don't do this to me!"

"Shut it up. I ain't trynna hear shit you got to say. But don't worry, I'ma make this short and sweet." With that said, he slapped Bonita across the face several times. She fell down and rolled into a fetal position. Batman continued to strike her. She covered her face with her arms and screamed for Batman to stop. When suddenly he stopped and she heard several shots ring out into the air and then heard something drop to the floor. Bonita was snatched off the floor and pushed hard into the wall. She opened her eyes to find that Batman had riddled Whizzie's body with a barrage of gun spray. Whizzie tried to play hero and was blasted to hell. Bonita screamed as loud as she could and then her world became dark. She slumped against the wall and slowly slid down onto the floor.

CHERRY BOMB

"Cherry, we always have such a good time together. You're my favorite cousin!" Aniya giggled.

"Girl, I'm your only cousin!" Cherry laughed. They were at Arundel Mills Mall sitting in the food court throwing down on some Bourbon chicken. Several large bags from various stores sat on seats next to them. Aniya and Cherry were first cousins and loved each other like sisters. Their mother's were siblings. Aniya stopped chewing and kicked her cousin under the table.

"Oww, why you kick me like that?" Cherry whined.

Aniya's eyes got big and she whispered, "Girl, Tommie and his boys are walking over this way. They ain't seen us yet, but I'ma make sure they do." Aniya stated.

"Girl, please don't put yourself on blast. I really don't…." before Cherry could finish her plea; Aniya stood up and waved her hands in the air while yelling Tommie's name, halfway across the food court.

"Yo, ain't that the girl from over on Lord Baltimore?" Tommie's boy said as he tapped Tommie who was leaning against the rail. Tommie turned to face where his boy was pointing. He looked over at the table where Cherry was sitting with her hands covering her face, while Aniya was waving like she was signaling a jumbo jet to land.

"Yeah, that look's like her. Come on, look like she wants us over there!"

"Girl, here they come." Aniya exclaimed excitedly.

"Aniya, why you do that? You know I can't stand Tommie or his boys! They always in shit and besides, that nigga ain't never got no money on nothing. All the girls say he's stingy and he makes them pay for their date. I can't believe you called that punk over here." Cherry complained.

"Oh, stop it, Cherry!" Aniya chastised. "He don't want you anyway. He's been looking my way for a minute. I wouldn't give him no playtime, but I'm about to see what's up now. And don't worry about me because I ain't paying for shit. If that nigga wants to play in my courtyard, he's gonna have to buy all new balls." She neck rolled. Cherry watched Tommie and his boys slither up to their table and saw the ridiculous smile that spread across her cousin's face. Cherry rolled her eyes and clutched her tongue.

"Uhmp," she said to herself and turned her back towards them.

"What's good, ma?" Tommie said to Aniya.

"Everything's good here!" Aniya responded seductively.

Tommie cocked his head and looked Aniya up and down. "I bet it is." Tommie said never taking his eyes off of Aniya. All thirty-two of her teeth were brightly shining. "Who dat?" Tommie said nodding his head at Cherry who refused to acknowledge their presence. She pretended to be engrossed with the people across the table from her.

Aniya hit her cousin on the shoulder and made a face at her. "This is my cousin Cherry." Aniya said giving her the evil eye.

"And this is my boy Lukie and my other partner Blick." Tommie introduced. Cherry gave a quick wave of her hand and went back to pretending they weren't standing there. Lukie was not to be put off. He liked what he saw and was determined to have a conversation with Cherry whether she liked it or not. He sat down directly in the seat in front of her.

Cherry's face contorted in disdain. "Ain't nobody tell you to sit down." She huffed.

"They didn't have to tell me shit. The seat was empty so I sat down. What, you don't want me sitting here?" He asked.

"No. I would prefer if you and your classless crew would take your asses back to where ya'll came from. I was fine by myself."

"Well, if you ask me, seem like your cousin and my boy over there don't feel that way." Cherry cast her eyes towards Aniya and Tommie who had stepped away from the table and were holding court over by the children's merry-go-round. Cherry sucked her teeth and scowled again.

"You know you shouldn't do your face like that. It might stay that way." Lukie chided.

Cherry let out a long loud sigh before she responded. "Really, that's the dumbest shit I've ever heard. That was so childish."

Lukie let the comment slide. "I'm just saying, you're such a pretty girl. Why you wanna look so ugly when you make those types of faces?" Cherry shifted in her seat.

She caught Lukie's comment about her being pretty but she wasn't giving into Lukie. She knew of Lukie and his boys. All the girls in the neighborhood and the surrounding hood areas talked about how much of a playa Lukie and Tommie were. She didn't know much about Blick. So she couldn't call it with him. Besides, he was in the line at Popeye's, which was fine with her, and she didn't want him coming back to the table either.

"Look, Lukie, let me cut through the chase. I know all about you and your playboy friend over there," she said pointing to Tommie. "And I don't want to be your new "gossip girl". You ain't gonna be talking about me and shit and have my business all over the hood. Hell to the naw!" she affirmed.

"Look, shawty, damn whatcha heard. All that talk is hater talk. Them bitches just be mad cause they can't get with me. I'm particular about who's in my circle and much more particular about who's in my bed. Stop listening to all that bullshit. Them bitches don't know me like that. Ask any of 'em you hearing that shit from if they ever been in my bed. No, wait ask 'em this, have they ever even been in my car. 'Cause if they ain't been in my car then they definitely ain't been with me!" he declared.

Cherry didn't respond. Instead, she looked Lukie in the eyes. She could tell he was telling her the truth. In all of five seconds, she saw his baby face features. Small almond eyes, thick eye lashes, thick eyebrows, a small scar on the left side of his face, probably happened when he was a little boy, a dimpled chin, a very thin mustache, smooth caramel skin and wavy brownish black low cut hair. She surmised he probably put on a do rag at night to keep them waves as tight as they were. She turned her face away to keep the "I am King" cologne he was wearing from jumping up her nose and making her twitch in her seat.

Lukie reared back in his chair, locked his arms across his chest and stared at Cherry. She was beautiful to him. She was a slightly thicker girl than most he had been with before. Her locs were neatly pulled back off her face and wrapped in a colorful scarf. Her large round eyes were soft and pretty. Her lips were full and thick, just like he liked them. The only make up applied was a thin coat of mascara and clear lip-gloss. Lukie inhaled the "Blvgari Noir" perfume that wafted over to him each time Cherry moved. He liked Cherry. He knew she was untainted and she was smart. He kept his eye on her. He asked around about her but none of his boys could say they hit that. He was going to make Cherry his. Now if only he could crack that hard ass exterior wall she was trying to put up. Fuck it. He was going to ask her out and he wasn't taking no for an answer. He leaned forward.

"Shawty, why don't you let me take you out to the movies or something like that."

Cherry turned and faced Lukie. "Why would I ever do that?" she asked.

"Because you like me and I like you. That's what two people do when they like each other. They go out and get to know one another."

Lord, who told this boy I liked him? Didn't nobody say shit about liking anyone!" Cherry thought. "Look, Lukie. I don't like you and I don't want to get to know you. I don't want or need no thug nigga trying to push all up on me. And besides, you can have any of them girls from Woodlawn, Pikesville, Owings Mills, Cockeysville, Towson and anywhere else you want. I keep telling you, I ain't trynna be your "gossip girl!" You won't be talking shit on me!"

"Yeah, you like me. I can feel it." Lukie laughed. He stood up, walked over to Cherry, grabbed her face and kissed her. Cherry tried to react but by the time she did, Lukie was walking away. Several minutes later, Aniya came floating back to the table.

"Girl, ain't Tommie fine? I should have gotten with that brother a long time ago. That's okay, cause I sure got his number now. Them other hoes can move out the way! I'ma have his shit on deadbolt!" she stated. "Oh, and I gave Lukie your number. He said he was going to call you later. We are all supposed to double date." Aniya said picking up her bags from the chair.

"What in the Sam hell did you do that for? If I wanted that nigga to have my number I would have given it to him my damn self and besides, he didn't ask me for it." Cherry screeched and began snatching up her bags also.

"He said he forgot to ask you after you kissed him!"

"What! I didn't kiss that boy. He kissed me. See, there he goes telling lies already. That's exactly why I didn't want to talk to him, and your ass goes and gives up my damn digits. You should have asked me first, Aniya."

"I know you would have given him a false number. Stop being such a bitch, Cherry. Lukie likes you and I can see that you like him too."

"I do not like that boy. I don't even know him!" Cherry shouted.

"Yes, you do. Your lying right through your teeth."

"I am not lying, Aniya!"

"Yes you are, because when you lie, you don't look at me and your eyebrows curl together."

"They do not." Cherry corrected. "Well maybe, I don't look at you but my eyebrows, now that's some new shit!" Cherry laughed.

"Girl, you're stupid. Come on. We got double dates waiting on us later and we got new outfits. You're driving home cause I want to finish talking to Tommie!" Aniya shrilled like a junior high schooler as she handed the keys to her cousin. Moments later they were on Route 100 headed home laughing and giggling about Lukie and Tommie.

"Where's your mother. I've been trying to call her ass all day and I can't get an answer."

"I don't know, Aunt Betty. When I came home from the mall she was gone."

"Damn it. I hope she ain't out somewhere getting high again. Are you okay, baby?"

"Yes, Aunt Betty. You know I can take care of myself. Don't worry about ma; I'm sure she's okay. When she's done getting high, she'll come home." Cherry replied.

"Cherry, I'm sorry, baby. I don't understand how my sister is so messed up. She won't listen to anybody and won't get help. When she comes in please call me okay? And Cherry, you're a good daughter, especially for dealing with this."

"Yeah, I'll call you later, Aunt Betty." Cherry put the phone on the cradle.

She was used to this now. Her mother either came home in the wee morning hours or not at all for days on end. Her mother's actions were slowly killing Cherry's love for her. She cared for her mother and at the same time hated her. She glanced at the clock that was nailed on the wall. It read 9:00pm. She picked up the phone and placed a few calls. All of the answers came back the same. No one had seen her mother. She wasn't going to worry about her ass. Her mother was a grown woman and Cherry didn't need her for much else, other than for her mother to collect the monthly welfare check that came in to keep the roof over their heads. Although most time, Cherry had to still help pay the rent because her mother smoked up most the check. Cherry worked at a clothing boutique after school. She could sell anything. She would make her customers feel like they were the most beautiful women in the world, which is why Cherry was killing them with her commission checks.

Cherry felt a buzz on her hip. She slipped her iPhone out of the case and read the text message. It was from Lukie. It read, "*Hey Cherry. Hope your evening is as beautiful as you are. I have to cancel our double date tonight. Something came up that must be handled right away. I promise to make it up to you beautiful.*

Cherry shook her head and immediately called her cousin. Aniya answered on the first ring. Before Aniya could say hello, Cherry blurted out, "Girl, I told you that nigga wasn't about shit! I bet something better came up. I bet his ass is with someone else. And then he didn't even call. He just sent me a fuckin' text message. Lying ass nigga!" Cherry shouted into the phone.

"Cherry, slow down! What's wrong?" Aniya laughed.

"That damn Lukie is what's wrong. He cancelled the date. He said something came up and he can't see me tonight. Talkin' 'bout he'll call me later this week. Why did you even give him my damn number, Aniya?" Aniya was laughing so hard, she started coughing. "Stop fucking laughing, Aniya. This is not funny damn it!" Cherry angrily pleaded.

Through fits of laughter, Aniya jeered, "I thought you didn't like Lukie. For someone who didn't like the boy, you sure are acting all mad and shit! You already acting like you his girl and just got stood up!"

Aniya heard the click of the telephone and fell out laughing even more. She looked at her cell phone and sure enough Cherry had hung up on her. Cherry had to laugh at herself after she hung up with Aniya. Truth be told, she did find Lukie intriguing. But she was not going to be an easy target for him. He was going to have to put in work to even get to first base with her.

Cherry walked to the makeshift bookshelf of a plank of wood and two cinder blocks and grabbed a book. She got as comfortable as she could on the shabby couch, and opened up a novel she had been waiting to read entitled, *'Year of the Crack Mom'*. She loved all the books that the Cartel Publications put out. They were penning nothing but fire between the covers of their books.

Cherry had just got heavy into chapter four of the book when she was startled by a noise. Her breath caught in her throat as she eased off the couch and tiptoed to the window. From the side of the window, she slowly parted the blinds and peeped through them. Cherry couldn't see into the night and didn't want to fully pull back the blinds, to get a better look, so she tiptoed to the front door and placed her ear to it. When the door suddenly burst open and she was thrown several feet across the room. She got up and ran but her masked attacker was on her ass. She rounded the corner of the kitchen and her eyes maliciously searched for a weapon. Seeing a pan of oil on the stove, she reached for it and threw the cold oil on her attacker. Both she and the attacker went down in a puddle of slickness.

Cherry scrambled to get up, as did the attacker. The attacker grabbed her by her T-shirt and pulled her back. Cherry wielded the pan in the air and brought it down across her attacker's hands. The attacker lost the grip on her shirt and Cherry fled back into the living room. Her screams went on def ears. If anyone heard, they were not helping. Cherry tried running up the steps to the bedroom but the oil on her feet caused her to slip on the first step. Her body crashed heavily against the stairs knocking the air out of her chest. She pushed herself up with her hands but couldn't move. Her chest was on fire and she could not breathe. She looked back to see her attacker putting a rag over her nose and mouth. She fought back with as much effort as she could but it proved to be futile. Several seconds later, she was out cold. Her attacker placed a hood over her head, bound her feet and hands and picked her up. He put her over his shoulder like a sack of potatoes and left the apartment, limping but victorious.

STIC'S STACKS

"Aston, how long before he gets there?" Stic said into his phone. He listened for the answer from Aston. "Tell that motherfucker to bring his ass on. I want this done now!" Stic ended his call and punched in the numbers 2-4-7. Within two rings, it was answered. "Is everyone back from work and the crew gone?"

"Yes, they are in their rooms."

"What did you make for dinner?"

"One of your favorites, smothered pork chops, mashed potatoes, and sautéed spinach."

"Did you make dessert? You know I need my dessert!" Stic added.

"And you know this. You know I made my baby a dessert. I'll bring it over in a minute."

"I'm hungry, bring your ass on." Stic pressed the button to end the call. He lay across his bed smoking a blunt and sipping his brand of scotch, *Johnny Walker Blue Label*. Stic pulled heavily on the blunt, held in the smoke and then exhaled. The calmness that he was waiting for enveloped him and immediately put him at ease. He took another sip of scotch from his snifter and opened up his Armani silk robe. He closed his eyes and began to fondle his dick. Tonight his thoughts were on who was bringing his dinner, Dominitra. The more Stic thought about Dominitra, the harder his dick became. He ran his hand up and down his shaft and let out a low moan. He put the glass on the marble top nightstand and sunk further into his down covers. He spread eagle and continued stroking his dick. He needed Dominitra now. Not later. Fuck dinner.

Just as he was opening his eyes, Stic looked up to see Dominitra towering over him.

"Put that shit on the table and bring your fine ass here." Dominitra placed the tray on the table and walked over to the bed and snuggled up with Stic. Stic melted into Dominitra's strong arms.

"Damn you feel so good." Stic said. "I want you, babe. Get ready."

Dominitra pulled a condom out of the nightstand. He pulled the luxurious bed covers back and lay in the center of the bed. While they embraced they were hot and heavy all over each other. After the foreplay, Dominitra got on all fours. Stic opened a magnum condom and slipped it over his massively thick, long dick. He positioned himself behind Dominitra's ass before opening it and ran his tongue up and down. He was tossing Dominitra's salad. Moans could be heard in the lavishly furnished bedroom. Dominitra was on all fours and Stic placed his dick at the opening of Dominitra's ass. He grabbed Dominitra's hip and pushed his throbbing dick in Dominitra's smooth chocolate abyss. They moved in sync as Stic fucked Dominitra with long hard thrusts. Dominitra was jerking off his own dick. They rocked in perfect unison. They were grunting, groaning, sweating and having lustful sex. Just as fast as Stic was giving it, Dominitra was throwing his ass back. Stic placed his hand around Dominitra's neck and cuffed them. He gently squeezed his hands into a chokehold and continued to pound with no mercy. With each stroke, Stic tightened his grip around the neck of Dominitra and rode that ass. Dominitra knew Stic was close to his orgasm. Several more deep thrusts and Stic let a yell out as he came with a load from deep within his balls. When the last drop of cum was expelled, they lay in the bed exhausted.

"You got some good shit, Da!" Stic said.

Dominitra was one hundred and ninety pound, six foot and eight inches of all man but he was also very gay. His real name is Damon but when he dressed in drag, he called himself Dominitra. He was a fitness and nutrition guru and he met Stic at a health club where Stick worked out. Several conversations later, Stic moved Damon into his compound. They had an agreement that Damon agreed to and signed it with his life. He was in love with Stic and would do anything for him. The problem with Stic was he did not want an exclusive relationship with Damon. Stic had a hankering for both men and woman.

Stic got up off the bed. He was ready to eat the hefty plate of food that he brought in earlier. "Da, I need to eat. Where's my plate, yo?"

"Let me wash my hands and get it, babe." Dominitra quickly got up and washed his hands and returned to the bedroom with Stic's plate on a silver tray. He picked up a strawberry and plucked it in Stic's mouth. "You's my man and if them bitches don't know they better ask somebody. I will pull out my glock and get to lighting this place up in here like the fourth of July." Dominitra said rubbing Stic in the back, "I wish a bitch would think she--" Stic cut him off.

"Chill, Damon. Stop trippin'. Go get me some cake!" Damon jumped off the bed and went to get Stic a slice of cake.

Stic reached for one of three remotes and hit a few buttons. The eighty inch flat screen slowly crept up from within the floor. The recessed lights in the bedroom were taken down a few watts and the window shades automatically lowered. Stic sat up in the bed and ravished the food on his tray. He channel surfed until his phone buzzed interrupting his surfing. Begrudgingly, he answered it. "Yeah, talk!" Stic listened to the caller for several minutes before he left out a hearty laugh. "That's what the fuck is up. Give me twenty minutes and I'll be there." He tapped his cell phone to end the call and pushed away the remaining food. He dialed 2-4-7 on the house phone, which stood for twenty-four seven, and meant he better get somebody at his compound twenty-four hours a day, seven days a week.

"Yes, Stic, I'm on the way. I'm just putting some whipped cream on the cake." Damon said.

"I need to leave out for a few. Make sure the Pound is locked down. I'll be back later." Stic informed.

"Don't worry them fish tails ain't going nowhere. But where are you going?"

"Damon, you know goddamn well you don't need to be asking me where the fuck I'm going. What I tell you about that shit? Nigga, you just handle the business here!" Stic huffed.

"S'Cuse me. Damn, I didn't mean nothing by it. Why you acting like that? You know I worry about you, Stic when you out there in them streets."

Stic briefly softened his voice. "Sorry Da, but you know to stay outta of my business like that. I gotta go. I'll holla later." Stic hung up the phone and jumped in the shower.

He quickly washed and picked out a pair of True Religion jeans, an Ed Hardy button down shirt and a matching pair of Ed Hardy kicks. He finished off his attire with a few sprays of Ed Hardy's *Hearts and Dagger* cologne. He looked in the mirror and liked what was staring back at him, a light skinned, athletically built man. He pursed up his lips and smoothed out the neatly shaved moustache. He picked out a *Pittsburgh Steelers* baseball cap and placed it on his faded haircut. He was prematurely going bald on the top of his head, compliments of his missing in action father. Light grey eyes stared back at him. He smiled and his right chipped tooth gave him a tattered, yet roguish smile. He snatched up his keys and was out.

Thirty minutes later, Stic killed the engine to his *Jaguar XJL Super sport* and walked into another secret location. He put a key in the door and proceeded down a hallway and turned right. He lifted the gate to the elevator and got on. The elevator descended down into a secret shaft. The lighting was dim and close to none. Stic was all too familiar with this passage so much so, you could blindfold him and he knew where he was going. The narrow walkway was cold and uninviting. Beyond him were several different dirt pathways that lead to various places deeper underground. If one were to become lost, they were shit out of luck. It was damn near impossible to find your way out. Stic knew of this underground world ever since he was a little boy. He and several other boys used to play down there after school. Two things happened down in the cave like holes that changed Stic's life. One was that he received his first blowjob from another boy named Jamie while they were playing hide and seek.

Jamie followed Stic into his hiding place and fondled him. At first Stic was angry. He pushed Jamie and threatened to beat his ass, but Jamie told Stic that he knew Stic liked boys and if he didn't let Jamie do him, he was going to tell everyone at school that Stic was a faggot. Jamie pushed Stic down on the ground and commenced to giving Stic a blowjob that had Stic squealing like a girl. After Stic ejaculated in Jamie's mouth, Stic didn't know what to do and was scared Jamie would tell anyway, so he picked up a large rock and beat Jamie to death with it. Stic knew another way out and fled without being seen. At that moment, Stic became aware of his double sexuality and the second thing he became was a killer.

MONEY MAKER

The room was spic and span. There was no trace of Dawn or Whizzie. The walls and the floor were scrubbed clean. But that was to be expected. Stic had the entire room made from plastic material that could be washed down with a hose. And it didn't hurt that Batman was the original clean up man. Mr. Clean didn't have shit on him. Stic gave Batman a pound.

"Aston in there?" Stic said nodding towards another closed door opposite the room.

"Yeah and he brought the doc with him too. They're both in there." Batman responded. Stic opened the door.

"Mad chemist, what up?" He greeted the men.

"Dude!" Aston greeted Stic. Stic pointed at an older white man who was busying himself with putting bottles back in his bag. Aston whistled and the man looked towards him. He nodded his head indicating to the man to come over. "Stic, meet Dr. Moore. He's the best in the business." Dr. Moore stuck his hand out for Stic to shake it.

"No offense doc, but I don't shake nobody's hand." Stic said.

Dr. Moore pulled his hand back embarrassed. He cleared his throat and ran his left hand through his thin brown hair.

"See that's the shit, I'm talkin' 'bout. How you gonna put your hand in your greasy hair and then shake mine? Ain't no tellin' what the fuck is in your scalp. Shit you might have lice or sumptin'. Shit, white folks is good for lice and shit."

Dr. Moore took offense. "Young man, I assure you I don't have lice. I am a licensed medical professional and I take impeccable care of my body. Maybe you should have your own hair checked for ringworm. Black people are well known for ring worm." He retorted.

"Fuck you, doc!" Stic returned.

Dr. Moore ignored Stic's comment. He turned to Aston and said, "My work here is done. I have completed the task at hand. Here are the devices you will need. This didn't come cheap and neither did my work. Now I need payment."

"And a nigga need to make sure this shit is working and guaranteed." Stic contended. "So before you get anything, make it do what it's supposed to do."

"Very well." Dr. Moore said. He gave Stic a key fob like device. He showed Stic how to operate it.

Stic couldn't wait for the five-minute lesson to be over with. He was ready to try out the device. "Bring them in." Stic said to Batman.

Two minutes later two bodies were seated in two chairs in front of Stic, Dr. Moore and Aston. Batman removed the hood from one of the bodies. When Bonita saw who was seated with her, she screamed as loud as she could. But the duct tape over her mouth kept the scream buried deep within her. She tried to break free of the chair but stronger duct tape kept her arms and legs at bay.

Aston turned to the doctor, "Get your stuff together and give me a minute, doc."

Dr. Moore rubbed his chin. He didn't like the fact that he had to wait for payment and he certainly didn't want to be a part of whatever Stic had in mind at the moment. He was prepared in case something went the wrong way. He went back over to the table where his bag was and opened it. He pretended to be looking for something but secretly tucked his gun in his hand. He looked over his shoulder and saw Stic and Aston engaged in conversation. Dr. Moore took advantage of their backs being turned and put his gun inside his breast coat pocket. He closed his bag and waited.

"Dr. Moore is waiting to be paid." Aston said.

"I got his money. He can wait. I need to know if this shit works first before he raises up. I need a demo. Tell his ass to set it up." Stic demanded.

Several minutes later, Stic was satisfied with the demonstration that Dr. Moore provided. He gave Aston a small leather briefcase to give to the doctor. After Aston and Dr. Moore left, Stic told Moop to retrieve his money and to make sure Dr. Moore was not to be heard from anymore. He laughed at his own joke. Moop took his orders and left.

Stic took the device and hit the switch again. Bonita's body shook in seizure movements. Bonita was terrified. She thought for sure she was going to die at any minute. She had no control over the involuntary muscle movements. She knew that whatever Stic was holding in the palm of his hand was the controlling device for the pain that shot throughout her body that caused her body to move in short sporadic movements. It also caused her to black out after the episode subsided. Bonita began to choke on her on spit. In the nick of time, Stic ripped the duct tape from her mouth as she gagged and vomited on herself.

"You nasty bitch!" Stic yelled at her. "Bring over the other one!" he commanded. Batman left and came back with a hooded body. He laid the body on the floor in front of Bonita. Stic snatched the hood of the body and licked his lips. This was the prize he won. He kicked Bonita's chair. She didn't respond. Stic gave a finger signal and Batman snatched Bonita by her face and shook her. She opened her eyes. She had no more screaming left in her lungs and no more fight; that was until she looked to down and saw the body on the floor.

"Cherry, Cherry, baby! What are you going to do with my baby?" She questioned Stick. "Cherrrrry!" Bonita screamed.

"Tape that bitch's mouth back up while I explain this shit to her!"

Batman re-taped Bonita's mouth. Cherry was still unconscious as she lay on the ground. Bonita's eyes were wider than a CD and tears streamed down her face. She tried with all her might to be free of the constraints that held her. Stic touched the button on the device and Bonita instantly seized in the chair. When it was over, she was barely conscience. Her breathing was shallow and her heart slowed. Her head hung down low in her chest. Stic rolled up a blunt and sat down to smoke it.

"Wake that bitch up." Stic said as he passed the blunt to Batman.

Batman took a long hit of the weed and then took a bottle of water and poured it over Bonita's head. She opened her eyes and tried to focus. Batman passed the blunt back to Stic as Bonita looked up to see Stic standing in front of her blowing smoke in her face. Bonita moved her face to the side to avoid the smoke. Stic burst out laughing.

"Ain't this a bitch, you don't like my weed but you will smoke up a crypt of Mind Bend. You're fucking hilarious." Stic said.

Bonita didn't hear anything Stic said. Her mind and energy were focused on her daughter laying on the floor.

Stic taunted, "Remember when you couldn't pay for your drugs and you didn't want to play my game of Russian roulette? You remember don't you, Bonita?" he sneered. "And since your stank ass didn't play that game, we played 'Let's Make A Deal'. At that time, I said I would let you live if I could have your daughter. Well I've kept my end of the bargain. You are alive, Bonita and so is that phat ass daughter of yours. Now here's the *new* deal of the day, she's coming to work for me. I could use new pussy like hers. She is going to be my money maker." Stic nodded at Cherry.

"Batman, strip that thick piece of bacon!" Batman took off every piece of clothing that Cherry had on. She lay there butt naked. Stic knelt down beside Cherry and ran his hand over her firm ample breasts. Her body was flawless. She didn't have a mark on her. Stic's dick was harder than a plank of wood. He continued to run his fingers down her body stopping just above her waxed pussy. He looked at Bonita and smiled. He watched Bonita frantically shake her head no. Stic pushed his middle finger inside of Cherry. He was met with resistance. She was a virgin. This phat young thing that lay before him was a fucking virgin. He couldn't believe it. Stic raised up.

"Batman, wake her up and then wait for me outside."

"Whatcha want me to do with Bonita?"

"Make sure she can't get up. I'ma show her how a cherry is popped!" Stic laughed.

Batman took the smelling salts and placed them under Cherry's nose. Several seconds later, Cherry was up. Frightened, she tried to stand up. But her efforts were pointless as she was still bound from her capture from her house. She lay naked on the floor, wide eyed and scared when she looked up and saw her mother bound to the chair. She too began screaming behind her taped mouth. Stic watched as both women tried to get to one another. He had enough of their antics. He stood in front of Cherry. She tried to scoot away but she didn't get far. He held up the device in his hands in front of Bonita's face.

"Watch what happens when I press the magic button on this one." He pressed the button on the remote and Cherry immediately started to have the same convulsion movements that Bonita had just gone through. Cherry didn't know what was happening to her body. She came out of the seizure disoriented.

"You both have been implanted with a device that tracks your movements. That means there will be nowhere that either one of you can go or hide that I won't be able to find you. I call this 'keep that ass in check'! See this red button, if I press this bitch, it's a wrap for you both. I know I don't have to tell you two not to make the stupid mistake of telling anyone about this. The consequences of your actions will be deadly. Now to make sure you both understand what the fuck I just said let me demonstrate the power I have over you." Stic pressed the buttons on both remotes and Cherry and Bonita started to seizure again. When it was over, he snatched Cherry by her legs and dragged her to the middle of the floor.

From behind his back he removed his glock. He unsnapped the safety and made sure a bullet was in the chamber. He then placed the glock on the arm of a chair. Cherry lay on the floor in paralyzing fear. She watched Stic unbuckle his pants and remove them. She further watched him step out his boxers and stand over her. She looked up at her mother with fear and hate at the same time in her eyes. Stic stroked his dick as he looked down at Cherry laying between his legs. He needed to remove the duct tape from around her ankles. When he did, Cherry kicked Stic in the face. He fell back against one of the chairs and onto the floor. Embarrassed he ran over and snatched his glock and pointed it at Cherry.

"Make another move and I'll body your ass right now!" he hollered.

Bonita rocked feverously in her chair as she watched Stic point the gun at her daughter. He slowly lowered his body down on top of hers. He posted the glock up to her temple. Cherry looked Stic in the eyes and saw nothing but darkness. She had no doubt that he would pull the trigger on her. She wanted to live because she wanted to kill this man herself and then she wanted to kill her mother for putting her in this position. Cherry stopped moving and focused on the dim light that was swung like a pendulum overhead. She felt Stic feeling for the opening of her pussy with his dick. He found it and slowly pushed the head of his dick in her opening.

"Awww shit! I got me a virgin pussy. I'm about to burst that cherry, baby. I know this pussy about to be good. It ain't never had no dick until now."

With several hard thrusts, Stic had broken Cherry's hymen and was fucking her pussy like a grown woman's. Cherry refused to let him see her in pain. She kept her eyes fixated on the overhead light as Stic went about his business on top of her. He groped and squeezed her breasts as he humped her tightness. He licked the side of her face and tried to kiss Cherry but she refused to part her mouth. Cherry also refused to look at her mother. Bonita cried hysterically behind the tape. She was powerless as she watched Stic rape her only child.

A single tear slid down Cherry's face as she lies there while Stic beat up and bruised her virgin pussy. She felt Stic tighten up his ass and stroke her faster and harder and several seconds later he lay on top of her panting out of breath. He stopped moving. He kissed her on the forehead and told her she was officially his. He pulled the glock from her head, put the safety back on and rolled off of Cherry. A mixture of blood and semen was between her legs. He laughed and then looked at Bonita.

"Damn, Bonita, you didn't tell me you had a real virgin daughter. Shit the way the girls be talking about her, I thought she was experienced. I see now that you can't believe everything you hear." Stic snatched up his blue jeans and waltzed out the room.

He returned with Batman. Batman sniffed the air and then looked at Cherry. He knew Stic tapped that ass. He wanted some of that pussy but Stic already had it and he didn't dare go behind Stic. That was a cardinal sin to fuck with the same bitches that Stic fucked with. Stic thought of it as treason and would not hesitate to cap a nigga for it. Fuck that bitch. There were too many others out there that were safer for him than the one laying on the floor now zoned out.

"Untie her and give her back her shit to put on."

Batman took a hunting knife from around the case that neatly tucked in the small of his back and cut the duct tape that held Cherry's arms bound. He snatched the tape from her mouth and threw her clothes at her. Cherry was sticky and bloody but she wanted to cover her body up immediately. She winced in pain as she pulled her jeans on and shirt. Her ribs were still hurting from the fall she suffered earlier when she was running from Batman. Stic sat on in a plastic chair with his glock pointed at Cherry. Batman served as back up with his semi automatic weapon pointed at Cherry too.

"Sit down, Cherry!" Stic said.

Cherry was in so much pain that she couldn't sit. "I can't, I hurt too much" she whimpered.

"Sit your used ass down!" Stic said coldly.

Cherry gingerly sat in a chair facing Stic. Her mind was reeling from all that was happening. Not once did she look at her mother.

Stic pointed towards Bonita and said to Cherry, "Your trifling mother didn't have money to buy her drugs, so she made a deal with me. Her life for you. As you can see, your mother sold you out. Now you belong to me. I'll be around to collect what is mine in due time. In the meantime, both you and your sorry ass mother need to know what not to do if you both want to live. Ya'll know the code of street. No fucking 5-0 and I damn sure better not hear a word of this from anyone else. The tracking device is implanted within your body somewhere. If you find it and it's tampered with in any way, it will automatically trigger itself and you will have fucked your own selves making my job that much easier!" he cajoled.

For emphasis Stic pressed the button on the remote and again watched the seizure show. This time, both Bonita and Cherry passed out.

DEADLY SILENCE

Cherry woke up on the floor of her apartment. Groggy and discombobulated, she stood up trying to clear her head and get her bearings. She fell heavily onto the couch. She opened her eyes and refocused and things came into view. She quickly looked around the tattered apartment and saw her mother lying on the floor coming around too. Cherry sprung to her feet, jumped over her mother and darted up the stairs careful not to fall. She ran to her room and grabbed clothes off hangers and threw them on the bed. She didn't give a shit what she grabbed. She snatched up shoes and threw them on the bed too. She yanked open the middle dresser drawer and grabbed underwear and socks. She rummaged around under her bed and pulled out a suitcase. She expeditiously threw everything in the suitcase. She snatched her Gucci purse off the back of the door handle, snatched up the suitcase and flew down the steps. She ran smack into her mother. With hatred in her eyes Cherry stared at her mother. Immediately Bonita fell to the ground sobbing profusely.

"Cherry, please don't go. Please listen to me. I didn't sell you, baby and I didn't promise to give you to Stic. He threatened to kill me." She cried. Bonita grabbed her daughter's leg and held onto to it. Cherry kicked her mother's hand away and walked to the center of the room. Thoughts of taking the suitcase and beating her mother to death with it were the forefront of her thoughts. Bonita crawled over to where her daughter was and began to beg for forgiveness again.

When she again grabbed Cherry's legs, Cherry snapped. "Get your fucking hands off of me, bitch! You fucking dead head! You've been gone for four damn days, Ma. Count 'em, four fucking days. Not once did you call home and check on me. But that's par for the fucking course. You never check on me so what the fuck was I thinking."

"Cherry, listen to me please. Baby, I saved your life."

Cherry backed up in astonishment of her mother's statement. Her mouth hung open with disbelief. "What the fuck did just say? Ma, the only life your addicted ass saved was your own."

"Cherry, I am still your mother. Stop talking like that to me." Bonita said standing up now to face her daughter.

Bonita was not groveling any more. She was still the head bitch in charge up in this camp no matter what Cherry thought. Cherry faced off with her mother.

"That man raped me, Ma. He fucking raped me in front of you. Didn't you see that shit? How could you do me like this, Ma? I'm your daughter. You're supposed to love and protect me. Instead, you sold me for your drugs. And not only that, now I'm hooked up to some damn device that has control of my body. I feel like I'm in a fucking science fiction movie. Who does this to people?"

"He did me the same way, Cherry. I got the same device you have in you. The man threatened to kill us both if he didn't get what he wanted. Cherry, I'm so sorry. Please forgive me. Please, Cherry. I love you. You know I would never do anything to hurt you. I saved your life. Cherry. I saved your life!" Bonita sobbed again.

"Your drug habit is what caused this whole mess!" Cherry screamed back.

"Cherry, if I could have killed him I would have. I wanted to trade places with you, baby."

"I wish you would have! He hurt me! I will never be the same. And I blame you for this! I hate you. I want you to die!"

Bonita felt the air leave her chest. She felt lightheaded. This was just too much to take.

Cherry pushed past her mother and ran into the bathroom. She retrieved her cell phone from her purse and placed a call. "Aunt Betty, please come and get me right now. Please? Yes, she's home. She's fine but I need for you to come and get me. Pleaasssse!?" Cherry pleaded. When Betty said she was on her way, Cherry ended the call, dropped her phone back in her purse and turned on the cold water and splashed her face.

She dared not look in the mirror. She couldn't look at herself. She opened the door to find Bonita standing outside of it. Cherry sidestepped her mother. When she didn't see the suitcase she packed, she screamed at Bonita. "Where the fuck is my suitcase, Ma? Give it back to me!"

"Cherry, I want you to listen to me."

"Ma, I ain't listening to nothing you got to say. I just want my bag and I'm out." Cherry hollered.

"Cherry, I know that I have not been the best mother at times, but got damn it, I am still your mother and you will not disrespect me like this. I have been through a lot that you don't know the half of. I witnessed a girl shoot herself in the head and then I saw Whizzie get shot up right after that."

"They should have shot you! Then I wouldn't be indebted to a man that just raped me because my mother sold me to him for her drugs!" Cherry screamed. "Now give me my suitcase so I can get the fuck outta of here!"

"No, Cherry. I'm scared for you. Please don't go. We need to work this out for both our lives!" Bonita said snatching at Cherry's arm.

Cherry broke her mother's hold and raced to the kitchen, snatched open the kitchen drawer, breaking two of her nails and withdrew a knife. She ran back into the small living room at her mother.

"You crazy, child! What the hell are you doing, girl?" Bonita screamed as she moved to the left of her daughter's hand just as Cherry plunged the knife into her mother's shoulder. Cherry withdrew the knife and wielded it again in the air as Bonita fought back with her good arm but was no match for her daughter. They tussled back and forth. Bonita tried to fight off her daughter but she couldn't.

Cherry dropped her mother on the floor with a solid punch to her face. Bonita shook it off and scrambled to her feet. She snatched the lamp off the end table and used it to defend herself. Cherry swung the knife through the air trying to wedge it into any body part of Bonita's body. Bonita got close enough to swing the lamp and knock the knife out of Cherry's hand. She seized the moment to jump on her daughter and throw several hard punches that landed into Cherry's face and head. Fighting was the only sound that resonated throughout the apartment. Cherry managed to get one of her hands free and threw a punch in her mother's stomach. It was enough to stumble Bonita backwards momentarily.

Cherry eyed the knife, on the floor by the couch. Bonita and her daughter continued to swing wild punches at one another but at the same time, Cherry was backing her mother up near the couch. All she wanted was to get her hands back on the butcher knife. Today, she was going to jail and she didn't care. An opportunity came when both Cherry and her mother fell into the couch. Bonita's grasp broke and Cherry lunged for the knife. Looking like a woman possessed by the devil and with no further regard for her own life or her mother's Cherry raised the knife. Bonita didn't move. She waited for death. She deserved it after what she had done to her own daughter.

"Cherry, stop! Stop it right now! Stop!" Cherry's aunt's voice stopped her hand midair. Cherry felt her hand being grabbed and felt another pair of hands around her waist. Aniya grabbed Cherry's waist and pulled her back as her aunt Betty wrestled the knife from Cherry's hand.

"Oh my God! What is going on in here?" Betty asked looking between Cherry and her sister Bonita.

Bonita spoke out of breath, "Nothing, a misunderstanding is all!"

"A misunderstanding? Your daughter was standing over you on the couch getting ready to stab you with this knife. What the hell? You call that a misunderstanding? Cherry, what the hell is going on in here?" Betty looked at her sister lying on the couch bleeding. She turned to Cherry and screamed. "What kind of shit is that to do to your own mother? I can't believe you would do something like this. I ain't leaving until somebody tells me what the fuck is up or I'm calling the police my damn self and have both of your crazy asses locked the fuck up!"

"Nooo!" both Bonita and Cherry screamed like simulcast twins. Betty looked at Bonita and then at Cherry. Something was definitely amiss.

"I'm fine. This is just a flesh wound. Cherry didn't mean it. I did something that she has every right to be mad at me for."

"Well what the hell is it then? Please enlighten my ass!" Betty exclaimed.

"Betty, I said, I'm fine. Just take Cherry and let her stay with you for minute." Betty never dreamed in a million years that she would walk into her sister's home to find her niece trying to stab her own mother.

"I said I ain't leaving until I get some answers. When I came in here you were about to stab my sister. Thank God I had a spare key. Ain't no telling what the hell could have happened up in here! This is frightful. Cherry, I don't trust you and I definitely don't like the idea that maybe you were trying to kill my sister."

"Aunt Betty, please let this be! This is more than I can handle right now!" Cherry cried. Betty approached her sister. "Then you tell me what this is about."

"Betty, Cherry's right. We can't say what this is about. It would put both our lives in jeopardy."

"Does this have anything to do with drugs?" Betty asked.

"For God's sake's, Betty, let it go! Just take Cherry with you for a couple of days until this blows over." Bonita pleaded.

Betty huffed in defeat. "Well at least let me see the wound. You're bleeding like hell all over the couch. You might need stitches." She said reaching for Bonita's shoulder. Bonita quickly moved away from her sister's grasp. She put her hand up to her bleeding shoulder and sat up on the couch to face her sister.

"Betty, listen to me. I can't do anything about the situation with me and my daughter. So stop fucking asking us what is going on and just take her and go."

Betty threw daggers at Cherry and then at her sister. "For now, I will leave this alone." Betty never took her eyes off of her sister as she hollered over her shoulders, "Cherry, get your stuff."

Cherry looked at her mother for her suitcase and Bonita pointed to the back of the couch. Bonita stood up and Cherry moved the couch away from the wall and retrieved her suitcase. Betty shook her head at the madness she was surrounded with. Aniya was happy that her cousin was finally coming to stay with her. Secretly, she wished Cherry had cut up her aunt Bonita. She wasn't a good mother anyway and didn't deserve a daughter like Cherry.

Betty and Bonita watched Cherry open the door and leave without saying a word to anyone. Bonita ran up the stairs slamming the bedroom door without saying a word to anyone either. Betty and Aniya stood in silence for a brief moment trying to take in what they had just witnessed. Silence ushered them out the door.

COMPOUND MONEY

Stic drove down a dirt road about a quarter of a mile away from his house. When he got to his destination, he pulled out a set of keys that were different than his home keys. He opened the door and entered. He checked the kitchen and didn't see anyone. He proceeded to the back of the home where he heard a TV blaring. He got to the bedroom door on his right and opened it.

"Trailer Trash, what's up girl?" he said. Trailer ran to the door and opened her arms to receive a hug. Instead, all she got was pushed to the floor.

"Bitch, you know damn well, I ain't hugging your stank ass. Look at you. I bet you ain't done nothing all day but get high."

"No, daddy, I worked this morning!" she replied.

"You have a part this morning?" Stic asked.

"Yeah, me and Carnival." She said.

"Where is Carnival, in her room?"

"No, Dominitra took her and Tawni to the store. They needed a couple of things."

"Alright then. I'll be up in the office. Don't disturb me."

Trailer watched Stic leave. She finally got up off the floor and went over to the window and looked out. She wanted to leave but couldn't.

Stic went to his office. He opened the mahogany cabinet and pondered what to pour. He selected a vintage brandy and poured a healthy shot into a snifter. He slipped off his shoes and sat down in his over sized leather chair. He placed both of his size eleven's on the top of his desk. He took a long swig from the snifter, closed his eyes and thought about his life.

In just a few short months he had gone from rags to riches with the Mind Bend drug. Most of the money came from major weight buyers of his product. Stic didn't deal with the street in any way. He didn't go to college to deal on the street corner. That shit was for the dumb motherfuckers. You couldn't get rich that way. The money was in dealing weight. Stick took another swig of his drink and tapped his fingers on the desk. He wondered what role he was going to put Cherry in. He finally did what he really wanted to do and that was make X-rated movies. He funded the triple X-rated movies with some of the money from his many illegal endeavors. Stic hired his own professional camera crew to make the highly sought after and highly unusual porno movies. He had three movie stars that lived in the compound.

Trailer Trash was a big titty flat ass white girl whom Stic had hooked on Mind Bend. Trailer Trash was famous for having sex with animals and objects. Her movies sold well with perverted white men. Tawni was the ghetto diva that had an ass so big it looked deformed. It barely fit on a toilet seat. She was straight hood. The young wanna be rappers and singers fucked with Tawni. Her male actors and hardcore lesbians found her fascinating and loved to fuck her in that big ass. And then there was Carnival, the infamous midget who loved sucking dick because she could stand while doing it. Big Blue was Stic's and the girl's bodyguard. He used to wrestle in college until he was thrown off the team for breaking his opponents arm in several places after his opponent called him a fat black nigger. Big Blue mostly traveled with Stic and if the girls had a paying guest, he served as the guarantee that payment was made.

Damon/Dominitra spent his time between the main house and the compound. Stic entrusted Dominitra to look after the porn stars and ensure their asses were in the compound at all times. Dominitra was the mother of the house. He got along with everyone except for Tawni. They bumped heads on many occasions.

Dominitra sometimes had small parts in some of the films as the guest Drag Queen. When Dominitra dressed in drag, he dressed to the nines. RuPaul couldn't touch him. Dominitra was beautiful when he was beat and he didn't wear anything less than designer, from his thirty-five hundred dollar wigs and hairpieces to his three hundred dollar perfumes. Dominitra had every designer purse and shoes to match that would make Oprah jealous. To say that Dominitra wasn't a beautiful drag queen would be telling a lie. The problem Stic had with him was he was in love with Stic.

Stic didn't give two shakes about how Damon felt about him. All Stic wanted to do was fuck that ass when he felt like it and for Dominitra to take care of business like he was already doing. Stic had no love for Dominitra and even less love for Damon without the drag. As a matter of fact, Stic never loved any woman but his mother. When he saw that he could make a bitch do anything he wanted after he gave her Mind Bend, he lost respect for her. To him, all women were useless unless you could make money off their backs and that's exactly what he did.

Today at the shoot, Dominitra was his usual diva self, as he waltzed in flawless and made Tawni suck her teeth and roll her eyes. There was no need for them to leave the premises to shoot their movies. Stic's camera crew made all the necessary arrangements to make movies right on the compound. Stic had a full studio there that rivaled any major studio. Everything from clothing stations to hair and make up. It also had a fully stocked bar and pantry, a heated Jacuzzi and an indoor and outdoor pool. Sometimes they even went in the woods so Trailer Trash could shoot scenes where she would fuck a tree or fuck a rock.

Stic was in deep thought about Cherry. He couldn't wait for her to arrive at her new living quarters. He reached in his pocket and pulled out the tracking remote. He tapped a few buttons and was satisfied that both lights on the screen were green. Good, that meant they were still within range. It had been a few weeks since he last saw or heard from Bonita or Cherry. He heard Bonita was now smoking crack, which meant she was seeking out other drug dealers because he didn't sell or make crack. He also heard that

Cherry hadn't been seen at her house lately. Soon, it would be time to stop by Bonita's and check up on them especially his new star, Cherry. Yep, she would be his very soon.

NEW LOVE

Cherry and Lukie had been kicking it with each other over the past several weeks and Lukie was digging him some Cherry. He wanted to take her out somewhere nice today, so he invited her to take a leisurely drive down to the Naval Academy in Annapolis to visit one of his cousin's who was a midshipmen. Now they were sitting in Lukie's Honda Accord just over the Severn River bridge lookout point. Lukie put the paper filled cup of Hennessey and Coke in the cup holder and turned to face Cherry.

"So what's up, Cherry, talk to a nigga!" he said looking intently at her.

Cherry smiled slightly and answered, "Whatcha mean by that?"

"Don't be playing dumb. You know what I mean, shawty. When we gonna stop beating around the bush and let me get in that bush?" Lukie joked.

Cherry shifted in her seat. She knew that she could not keep putting Lukie off. She liked him but she was not ready to have sex with Lukie or anyone else right now. She placed a warm hand over Lukie's and stared out the window as he waited for her response. "Lukie, I'm not ready."

Lukie sat up in his seat and said, "I mean come on, shawty. We've been kickin' it for a minute. Shit, you ain't even letting me feel you. At least let me touch you then." Cherry dropped her head.

Lukie unbuckled his seat belt, opened the door and got out. He proceeded around to Cherry's door, opened it and told her to get out. Cherry's first thought was he was putting her out of his car.

"Lukie what are you doing?" She questioned nervously.

"Just get out." He replied.

Cherry reached for her purse, unbuckled her belt, opened her door and got out. She began to walk away from the car.

"Yo, where the fuck you going?" Lukie yelled.

"I'm going home. Isn't that why you told me to get the fuck out of your car? Because, I won't let you fuck me and shit, so you just gonna put me out." She yelled.

Lukie doubled over in laughter. "Girl, get your ass back over here. I didn't say shit about putting you out or asking your ass to walk nowhere. What the fuck is up with that? All I said was get out. You's a trip girl."

"So what are we getting out for?" Cherry asked, embarrassed.

"Whew, wait, I gotta catch my breath on that one." He said gulping for air. "You was about to go hard huh?" he said laughing again. "Where the hell was you walking to? Do you know how long it would have taken your ass to get back to Baltimore? Shit, three days!" He said doubling over in fits of amusement again. Cherry playfully punched Lukie in the arm. He reached out and pulled her close into his chest and wrapped his strong arms around her. They leaned against the car.

"That shit was not funny at all, Lukie. I thought for sure you was asking me to get out and start walking." She said nuzzling up under his chin. Lukie kissed the top of her forehead.

"Naw, shawty, I just wanted you to see the view. It's awesome. You can't get the realness of it sitting in the car, Cherry."

He pulled her face up to meet his gaze and kissed her softly. Cherry resisted at first but Lukie moved in slowly kissed her and then his tongue parted her soft lips and snaked in her mouth. His kiss was sensuously wet and hot. Lukie's mouth was like a vacuum and Cherry's mouth gave into the losing battle. She let her mouth do as it pleased as her tongue sought his; their kiss becoming more intense. Cherry felt Lukie's hands glide softly down the front of her shirt and massage her breasts. A moan escaped her mouth through the kiss. Lukie pressed his body harder against

Cherry's. His dick began to swell in his pants and Cherry felt it against her stomach. She tried to push herself away from him but found that her feet would not obey the command to move. Lukie sensed her hesitation. He held her tightly. They continued to kiss until Cherry's mind wandered back to the rape and suddenly she stopped Lukie and broke out of his embrace. With a look of confusion stamped on his face, Lukie shook his head.

"Cherry, what's wrong, boo? What's going on with you? Every time we get close like this you pull away. Is someone else hitting that poonani?"

Cherry turned away from Lukie. She didn't want him to see the pain in her eyes and she didn't want him to drag the truth from her. Lukie took her silence as a confirmation. He instantly was heated. He snatched her by the elbow and turned her around to face him.

Nostrils flaring, he asked, "So you telling me that all this time, I been romancing your ass, you been fucking another nigga? Huh? That's why I can't get none, Cherry?"

Cherry stared back into Lukie's face and became enraged that he would think that of her. She extricated herself from his grasp and walked to the car. Lukie quickly beat her to the car door and stood in front of it, preventing Cherry from opening it.

"Cherry, who the fuck is the nigga you fuckin' with and ain't telling me?" he hollered.

"Lukie, I ain't fucking with nobody. That's your dumb ass putting stupid thoughts into your own mind and words in my mouth. I ain't never said nothing about another man!" She snapped back.

"Well your ass didn't exactly say you didn't have one either. So what gives, Cherry?"

Sadness overcame her. With everything she had, she tried not to cry but her tears defied her wishes and slowly crept down her cheeks. Lukie didn't know what to say or do. He hadn't expected Cherry to cry and what was she crying about? Concern now took over where anger was. Softly, Lukie asked Cherry what was wrong.

She shook her head and reframed from answering. Cherry was in love with Lukie and she didn't want to hurt him. She also knew Lukie was a hot head who would go off at the drop of a hat. If she told Lukie anything about the rape, he and his goons would be in the street with guns a blazing. Besides, she was still implanted with that seizure device and had no doubt that Stic's crazy ass would jump through hell with gasoline drawers, just to push the button to see her convulse and die. She shook the thoughts from her head and answered Lukie.

"It's complicated and it has to do with my mother and I can't talk to anyone about it right now."

"Come on, shawty, it can't be that bad. Talk to me. You know I got your back, boo. Tell me what's up?" He pried.

"Lukie, I can't. I promised my mother that I would not talk about her drug habit." Cherry lied.

"So this is *really* about your mother?" he asked.

"Yes."

Lukie considered her explanation. Truly he was not at all convinced that this was about her mother. So he pressed for more information. "Cherry, have you noticed that every time we get close to knocking boots, you freeze up and zone out on me? Does that have anything to do with your mother too?"

Cherry shifted from her right to left foot and slowly answered Lukie with a yes. Lukie went to open his mouth for more questioning when Cherry surprised herself and Lukie as she slammed her mouth down over his. This shut him up and he forced her back onto the car door. Lukie was the one to break the kiss this time. He gently lifted Cherry's face and peered into her eyes looking for answers that she was not able or unwilling to give. He thought it was time he told her.

"Cherry, you know I love you." He half asked, half stated.

Cherry blinked back tears again as she told him that she loved him too. Lukie swiped the tears from her face and kissed her again. Cherry's body was beginning to feel some sort of way that she had not experienced before. With the kiss becoming more intense, Lukie began to grind himself against Cherry again. She decided to let herself go. She stepped back and looked at Lukie. "Take me to a hotel."

With eyes wide and his dick standing up through his pants like a pole posting up a tent, he whispered, "Are you sure, boo?"

Cherry took his hand and placed it over her heart.

"I love you, Lukie and you said you love me too, right?"

"Yes, Cherry. I loved you since the first time we went out. I was just scared to tell you."

"Well take me with you tonight."

Thirty minutes later, they were at the Loews Hotel in Annapolis Maryland checking in. Cherry walked into the luxury suite and sat down on the couch. She was nervous and now wondered if she was ready for this. All kind of rampant thoughts raced through her mind. Maybe this was too soon. What if all he wants is to get me in the bed? Does he really love me? What the fuck am I doing here! Why did I even agree to this?

"Yo, Cherry, you okay, babe? Didn't you hear me calling your name?" Lukie said handing Cherry a glass of wine.

"No, I'm sorry, Lukie. I guess I was thinking about something." She said taking the wine glass and sipping from it.

"That's what I'm talking about, boo. You just seem to go into a place that I can't reach." He watched her take another sip of wine. "Be cool with that. I know you ain't much of a drinker, but it will help calm yourself. 'Cause I know you all nervous and shit. But ain't nothing to be nervous about, Cherry. I love you and ain't gonna hurt you, babe." Cherry didn't respond. Instead she looked around the fancy suite that Lukie had just plucked down four hundred dollars for the night. It included the fully stocked mini bar that Lukie was happily helping himself too.

With Hennessey and Coke in his glass, he sat down next to Cherry on the couch. He grabbed the remote and turned on the radio to WHUR. An old ballad from Maxwell crooned them both. Lukie sat back comfortably in the deep soft cushion and waited for

Cherry to follow suit. When she continued to sit rigidly on the each of the couch, he set his drink down and gently pulled her back into his arms. He allowed her to take a couple more sips from her wine before he took it from her hands and placed it on the table next to his. He turned her towards him and waited for a sign. Several moments later, they were locked in a kiss on the couch.

Lukie was gentle and slow in his foreplay with Cherry. He didn't want to take the chance of her zoning out on him again or stopping the action. Cherry let Lukie take her top and bra off. He massaged her breasts causing her nipples to stand up like little mountains. Cherry didn't know how to react in her mind but her body knew how to react to Lukie's touch. He continued taking off her remaining clothes. When she was in nothing but her boy shorts, Lukie pulled her up from the couch and took her to the bedroom. He snatched back the covers and waited for Cherry to climb into the bed. Naked, they both huddled together under the warmth of the covers. Lukie continued his foreplay of kissing, massaging and touching Cherry all over her body. He took Cherry's hand and put it over his dick. Cherry's hand immediately withdrew. Her eyes were as huge as saucers. He chuckled.

"Didn't know I was packing like this did you?" he said proudly cupping his entire nine-inch Mandingo dick.

"I know you ain't about to put that in me?" she said.

"Hell yeah, I am. What you want me to do with it, cut half off?"

"Lukie…" Cherry stammered, "I don't know about this. Please don't hurt me." Lukie sat up on his elbow and looked at Cherry. He could see the fear in her eyes. This was something he had not seen before. He was puzzled now.

"Cherry, I ain't gonna hurt you, baby. This is making love, boo. This ain't sexing tonight. This is our first time and I want to make love to you. Let me do that okay?"

Cherry's mind was no longer with being with Lukie. All she felt was an urgency to get out the bed and run into the next room. She didn't want Lukie touching her anymore.

"Cherry, relax, baby. I got you." He assured.

But the way Cherry was now responding made Lukie wonder if he should just wait. He stopped caressing Cherry and sat up and looked at her. Cherry was rigid again. She looked like she was frozen stiff. Lukie didn't want her this way. He wanted Cherry to give herself to him without reservation. He swung his feet over the side of the bed, picked his jeans up and slid into them. He walked around to the other side of the bed and kneeled down beside her. He took her soft hand into his.

"Baby, we can wait. I don't want you to do this unless you're ready and you're not ready, Cherry." He softly said. Cherry saw the sincerity in his eyes. Lukie pulled the covers over her breasts.

"Put your clothes back on and come join me." He raised up and swiftly turned. Before Cherry could blink, he was gone. She quickly sat up in the bed and wiped a tear that fell from her eye. She pushed herself out the bed, snatched up her clothes and quickly put them on. She hesitated when she got to the door. She looked out and saw Lukie sitting on the couch, drink in hand, looking directly at her in the doorway.

He patted the couch beside him indicating for her to come and sit beside him. Cherry obliged. When she sat down, Lukie immediately pulled her closer to him. Cherry leaned in and placed her head on his shoulder. The only sound that resonated was Lukie sipping his Hennessey and Coke. When he finished, he placed the glass on the coffee table and turned towards Cherry. She avoided his stare by looking down at her hands. Lukie lifted her face and forced her to meet his gaze.

She spoke first. "Lukie, please don't be mad. I thought I was ready for this but I'm not. I wasn't trying to play you or no shit like that, honestly. Please believe me." She pleaded.

Lukie let her statement linger in the air between them before he responded. "I believe you, Cherry and I'm cool with it. Let's just chill and enjoy these drinks because this room and the mini bar costing' my ass a grip right now. I could have done something else with the money." Cherry was uneasy with Lukie's statement but resigned to keep her mouth shut.

Several drinks later, Lukie was fast asleep on the couch. Cherry moved to the other end of the couch and balled up. She was ready to go home. She whipped out her phone and texted Aniya.

An hour later, Cherry was safely in Aniya's car headed home. She prayed after Lukie woke up and read her note, he wouldn't be mad that she left. All the way home, thoughts of the rape played over and over in Cherry's mind. It had been weeks since the rape happened but it was still a very vivid reflection for Cherry. She had not talked to or seen her mother in all that time. Bonita called but Cherry refused to speak with her. Secretly Cherry wished death would creep up on her and take her straight to hell.

Aniya had been talking non-stop since picking Cherry up. Cherry barely heard or paid attention to what her cousin was saying. Cherry's mind would not stop wondering what it would feel like to make love with her boyfriend and not be afraid. But because of how brutally her virginity was taken, she was now reclusive with her body and was always zoning out to block out the rape images and sounds of it every time they systematically entered her mind. Would she ever be able to let another man touch her? Cherry sank further into the car seat as she wondered what it would be like to have the power of life and death in her hands. Death wouldn't be evil enough for her mother and Stic and she prayed for nothing but death to both of them.

CHECK UP

Stic blew the pungent smoke out of his lungs. It swirled up in the air and was captured by the wind and taken to smoke heaven. He sniffed hard and passed the blunt to Moop. Skibop was in the back seat of the Chevy Magnum rolling up another blunt. This was the car that Stic liked to creep around town in to see the action without being seen. With the windows heavily tinted, visibility in the car was at zero percent. There were no rims on it so it looked like all other Magnums. The car sat quietly at the corner of Marriottsville and Bennett roads.

"Ain't that them?" Moop asked pointing. Stic knew that they were always together.

"Yeah, that would be them." Stic replied. A deadly silence wafted through the car as all eyes watched.

"When you wanna do this, Stic?" Moop asked.

Stic didn't answer. Instead he put up his forefinger and silence once again filled the car. Stic rolled down the passenger side window and stuck his head out.

"So what movie are we going to see tonight, boo?" Aniya asked her boyfriend on the phone. "Oh hell no. You know I don't do no damn scary ass movies. I don't want to see that! Okay, hold on, while I ask her." Aniya turned to Cherry.

"Tommie, wants to know what you want to see tonight and don't be saying a horror flick cause you know I ain't down with it."

Cherry was taking bags out of the back seat of Aniya's car. She rolled her eyes at Aniya and laughed. "I don't care. Me and Lukie are hanging with ya'll tonight, so it's ya'lls decision."

Aniya continued her conversation with Tommie as Cherry continued to unload the car. Cherry popped the trunk open and snatched a Wal-Mart bag out. She closed the trunk and out of routine looked down the street. She didn't like what she saw. She dropped the bag and ran over to Aniya, strongly grabbing her by the arm. Her voice was barely audible as she stammered through her instructions to her cousin.

"Aniya, let's go. Come on, girl, get in the house." Aniya resisted Cherry's plea and snatched her arm out of Cherry's grasp.

Mortified, at what she saw, Cherry hollered as she pulled and pushed Aniya towards the front steps. "I…I…we have to…"

"Cherry, girl, what the hell are you talking about and why are you pushing me up the damn steps. You trying to kill me or something? Stop it, Cherry! I'm on the phone!"

"Aniya!" Cherry screamed, "Get your ass up the steps right now and in the house! We ain't safe out here right now! Come the fuck on!"

Cherry grabbed Aniya by the arm and practically pulled it out of its socket as she jerked Aniya up the steps. Cherry was handling Aniya so hard, that Cherry tripped up two of the steps stubbing her foot on the last one causing her and Aniya to plummet. Cherry pushed her cousin off her.

"Get up, Aniya, come on!" Cherry winced in pain from her stubbed toe as she hobbled to an upright position.

"Damn it, Cherry, you made me put a hole in my new jeans." Aniya huffed. "Stop it! You're acting crazy! What's wrong with you?"

Cherry looked down the street and saw Stic looking out the car window back at her. She turned on her heels and headed towards the porch, leaving Aniya behind.

Stic had watched a visibly scared Cherry pushing her cousin up the steps. He laughed out loud at seeing her in a panicked state. "Want to see her dance?" Stic asked no one in particular in the car.

"Yeah, man, make her do the shake." Skibop snickered.

"Man, I bet if I gave that bitch my dick to suck and pressed the button, I bet that would be some awesome head." Moop said.

Skibop turned around in the seat and looked at Moop. "Motherfucker, is you just fuckin' dumb like that? If you put your dick in her mouth and press that button, you ain't gonna have no dick, stupid ass. She damn sure is gonna bite that motherfucker off while she's having convulsions or don't you think like that?" Skibop sucked his teeth and turned back around. "What's wrong with him, Stic?" Skibop asked.

Embarrassed and not to be the brunt of the joke, Moop replied, "You just mad cause you and Batman wanted to hit that ass and Stic got to it and broke it in first. You be at home wacking your shit cause you be thinking about that virgin pussy."

"Fuck you, Moop! Ain't nobody said shit about hitting that!" Skibop retorted. He was heated.

"Naw, nigga, that ain't what you said. You was mad cause you and Batman bet on who was gonna tap that ass first and when Stic got it, and pissed you off. 'Member you said, that Stic always takes the best ass for himself." Moop stated adding more fuel to the fire that was about to erupt in the car.

Stic didn't utter a word as he heard the exchange between his two soldiers. He watched both of them in the rearview mirror.

"You know what, Moop? You got a fuckin' big ass mouth. I was just talking shit with you. Why you got to go and put me and Batman out there like that? Shit, nigga, you worse than a bitch! Fuck you! You ain't got to ever worry about me saying shit else to your stupid ass again. Stupid ass motherfucker!"

"No fuck you, Skibop. I ain't gonna be too many more of your stupid motherfucker's either. You need to watch that shit, nigga." Moop shot back.

Enlightened by their remarks to one another yet tired of them acting like bitches, Stic told both of them to shut the fuck up. Like reprimanded children, they began to sulk. Stic reached in his pocket and retrieved his device. "Now you too bonehead mother-fuckers watch and see the power I can have over anybody and I mean anybody." He emphasized looking at each of them. Satisfied that Moop and Skibop both understood what he was saying, Stic turned his attention back towards Cherry and Aniya who were almost on the porch. Stic hit one of the buttons on his device.

Aniya watched horrified as Cherry suddenly stopped and stood perfectly planted on the last step convulsing in jerk like spurts. "Cherry, Cherry, Cherry…Oh my God…Oh My God,…Cherry!" Aniya screamed at the top of her lungs. Aniya went to reach for Cherry when she stopped convulsing and fell to her knees like someone punched her. Disoriented and drained, Cherry tried to get up but fell back down on her hands and knees. Aniya immediately dropped beside her cousin.

"Cherry, be still. You just had a seizure. Oh my God, Cherry, you didn't tell me that you have seizures. I'm calling the ambulance right now. You have to get to the hospital." Aniya shrieked.

Cherry saw the phone in Aniya's hand and with all her strength reached over and slapped it out.

"What the hell are you doing, Cherry? Why did you do that? What is wrong with you?" Aniya quizzed.

"See that car down there!" Cherry said, indicating the car with a slight nod of her head. "A drug dealer that my mother fucks with is in there!" she continued.

Aniya looked at the car. "That man ain't coming down here for us. Look at him." Aniya pointed at Stic's car. "He's just sitting there! What the hell does he have to do with us?" She barked.

"For Christ's sakes, just help me get in the house please."

"But what is going on?"

"Aniya and don't question me. Just trust me, okay?"

Aniya hurriedly pulled the key out of her pocket, helped her cousin to her feet and walked her to the door. When the key turned the lock and the door was opened, both girls fell through it. Cherry slammed it shut and engaged the deadbolt lock. She hobbled over to the window and slowly pulled back the curtain just enough to peek out.

Aniya was scared. She had never seen Cherry act this way and knew something was wrong. Aniya raced to the back door and double-checked the door making sure it was locked. "Cherry," she whispered, "What is going on? Girl, you got me scared ass shit!"

Cherry didn't answer as she watched Stic get out of the car and stand beside it. He was looking up at the house. Cherry's hands shook as she held the curtain back. Stic began walking towards the house and Cherry panicked. "Oh my God, he's coming this way. Aniya, get a knife!" She screamed.

Aniya didn't need coaxing. She ran into the kitchen and grabbed two knives. Cherry snatched one out of her hands and looked back through the window. The car was still there but Stic was not. Overwhelmed with fear Cherry ran over to the door and stood behind it.

"Cherry, I'm calling the police right now." Aniya whispered.

"Noooo, don't call them, Aniya. If you do, it will cost me my life. Put that damn phone down right now and get over here."

Petrified, Aniya ran over to Cherry's side. Both girls stood behind the door with knives in the air waiting for their attacker to enter. After several minutes, when Stic didn't kick the door in or even try the doorknob, Cherry crept back to the window. Slowly she opened the curtain just enough to see Stic's car still parked at the corner and a police car pulled up behind it. Immediately, Cherry screamed at Aniya. "Did you call the police after I told you not to!?"

"Hell no, you saw me put my phone back in my pocket, Cherry."

"Well, the fucking police are out there!"

Aniya was peeking out from over top of Cherry's shoulder. They watched as Stic got out of the car and then gave the police officer some dap. Laughs were shared between the officer and Stic and then the police car pulled off. Stic looked back at the house and momentarily hesitated before getting back into the Magnum and speeding off. Cherry sank to the floor in a frightened crumpled heap.

Aniya snatched Cherry by her arms and shook her. "God-damn it, Cherry, what the fuck was that about? What danger are you in or running from? Tell me now, Cherry?"

Cherry snapped herself out of her cousin's grasp. She stood up with the knife in her hand. Instantly, Aniya was transported back to the night, she and her mother came in to Cherry's home only to find Cherry standing over her own mother with a knife ready to strike. Aniya stepped back. Cherry saw the fear in her cousin's eyes and realized she was still clutching the knife. She dropped it on the floor and ran to the bedroom with Aniya on her heels.

RED LIGHT VIOLATION

Stic and his boys were still laughing at the way Cherry's body reacted to the seizure dance that Stic inflicted on her. They stopped at a local bar called, "Sista's Place", to throw back a couple of shots and find some new bitches for the night.

Skibop wanted his dick sucked and immediately thought about Carnival but after being put on blast by Moop, he knew asking Stic to come out to the compound was out of the question. He was gonna tighten Moop up for that shit when he got him alone. Several drinks and several hours later, Stic and his crew jumped in their ride and sped off the parking lot.

"Mom, are you anywhere near the market? I just got in the house and don't want to go back out. Can you bring me a couple of things?" Aniya asked her on the phone.

"What do you need?" Betty inquired while trying to find a pen as she ran the red light causing the driver of the Magnum to swerve.

"Baby, I got to get off the phone. I just ran the light. I'll call you once I get in the store and you can tell me what you want then." Betty said as she looked back in the rearview mirror and blinked as the owner of the Magnum turned around and was gaining on her.

"Oh shit!" Betty said out loud.

She was praying that the driver of the Magnum made a directional mistake that caused it to turn around. She cautiously lifted her eyes again to the rearview mirror and noticed the car was directly behind her. Her fingers gripped the steering wheel causing the blood flow to her hands to cut off as they slowly became numb and fear gripped her heart. Betty reached for her cell phone again. She was ready to hit the famous 9-1-1 numbers when she had to stop at the next red light.

The Magnum took full advantage of no other cars in the lane to her right and pulled up beside her. Betty brought the phone to her ear in the pretense of speaking with someone. The Magnum's driver's side blacked out window slowly crept down. A nine-millimeter subcompact Glock 26 was pointed directly at her. The sudden fear of being shot stopped any foot movement on the gas pedal. The motion of the gun to roll down her window made her do just that. A thin face that was hidden behind a pair Versace sunglasses, sat up into view.

"Yo, bitch, you trynna kill a nigga back there or some shit? What the fuck was that about?" Betty couldn't find her voice. "Yo, you hear me talking to your ass? You deaf or sumthin'? I'ma ask your ass again, what the fuck was you doing back there? Your ass ran the damn red light and almost ran into my shit. Is you crazy or on drugs?

"Oh, I know what it was, it's that damn cell phone. You bitches can't stop running your fuckin' mouths for two fuckin' minutes. You can't even drive that piece of shit without talking on the motherfuckin' cell phone. Put that fuckin' phone away when you driving through my area. You heard?" he shouted through his window.

"I'm sorry. I didn't realize I had run the light until it was too late. It won't happen again." Betty said.

Stic sniffed and then hock spit out his window. He raised his hammer again in view and said, "Yeah, I know it ain't gonna happen again, cause I'ma make sure it don't. I--" he was cut off of his threat by Skibop tapping him.

"Stic, I just got some info man. We got a situation. Let that bitch go. We gotta handle shit elsewhere." Stic stared back at Betty and lowered his gun. She hadn't realized that she had been holding her breath. Stic's car window slowly shut. The car drove off with a sense of urgency leaving tire marks where the Magnum previously rested.

Betty let out a loud sigh and nervously pushed the gas pedal. She was too nervous to drive any further so she pulled over to the side of the road. She laid her head on the steering wheel and willed her heart to slow down. When it she was calm enough, she called her daughter and told Aniya that she didn't feel like going to the market. She wasn't going to tell Aniya or Cherry about the incident because she didn't want them to worry. But in her mind she wondered if she should report what just happened to the police. And then the code of the street barreled through her head. Her answer was a definite no. She didn't want to take the chance of having a retaliatory example made out of her or the girls.

Aniya listened to her mother's uneasy voice over the phone. She also had problems and wanted to tell her about what happened earlier with Cherry but decided against it. Besides, Cherry begged Aniya not to say anything to anyone so for now, Aniya would keep her mouth shut and so did Betty. Secrets were becoming common between them.

SCARED SHUT IN

Aniya and Cherry were huddled up in the bedroom with the curtains pulled tight and the bedroom door locked. Cherry had been crying off and on.

"Cherry, please stop crying. Why won't you just tell me what's going on with you? Does this have anything to do with what happened at your house? And who was that drug dealer that you are obviously scared of?" Aniya asked.

Cherry sniffed back snot and wiped away her tears. She looked at her cousin and said, "Aniya, my mother ain't shit. That bitch let--" Cherry stopped mid sentence and broke into a deep sobbing cry.

Aniya sighed heavily. She could do nothing but pull her cousin into her bosom and rock her as she listened to her cries. Over the past several weeks, Cherry would break down and cry a lot, especially at night when she thought Aniya was sleeping. But Cherry could not and would not disclose what happened the night that Aniya saw her with the knife standing over her aunt Bonita. Aniya felt something terrible had happened to her cousin a few weeks ago and she wished Cherry would open up about it. Maybe she could help her if she only knew what the problem was.

Cherry didn't go out the house for almost a week after seeing Stic. Aniya tried to get her out but she refused to go. Even Lukie couldn't get her to go out with him. Lukie talked to Aniya on the phone and Aniya was not trying to get caught in the middle of telling Lukie a lie so she told Lukie he needed to see Cherry for himself and talk to her personally. He decided to follow Aniya's advice. He needed to know what the hell was going on with his girl and he needed to know now.

SIBLING STARE DOWN

Today, she was going to get some damn answers or there was going to be some moving of furniture. "Can I come in?" Betty asked from the doorway.

Bonita's grimaced face said it all at the sight of her sister. She wasn't trying to see her today, let alone let her ass in her house. Why didn't she look out the damn peephole before she opened the door? Bonita automatically assumed it was Frog coming back with some crack for them to smoke.

"I ain't leaving, so you might as well let me in or I'ma push my way in!" Betty snarled.

Bonita sucked her teeth and stepped aside. Betty walked into the apartment.

"What do you want, Betty? I got somewhere I need to be. You came at a bad time." She moved for the couch. "And don't go getting all comfortable and shit, cause I told you I've got to go somewhere!" Bonita hollered over her shoulder as she closed the door.

Betty sat down on the three-legged raggedy brown couch anyway. The leg on the front left side had come off and several bricks had been placed under it to steady it. Betty scanned her sister's apartment and shook her head at the living conditions. The apartment was smaller than her garage and Bonita was the worse housekeeper in the country. Clothes and shoes were thrown everywhere. Dishes were stacked in the kitchen sink and garbage was overflowing in the corner. Betty sucked her teeth as her eye caught site of a sanitary pad lying on the top covered with dry blood. She felt her skin crawling and quickly averted her eyes and stood up and brushed off her clothes.

Betty unleashed her disparagement of the nasty apartment out to her sister. "Look at the garbage with that nasty ass pad lying on the top of it. You didn't even have the common courtesy to wrap it up. Now that's just a trifling mess!" Betty condemned.

Bonita went over to the trash, pulled out the used sanitary pad and put it on the counter.

"Oh my God, Bonita, take that shit off the counter! Don't be so damn nasty!"

"I'm getting ready to wrap it up and give it to you as a present." Bonita retorted. She found a plastic bag and threw the used pad into it. She brought the bag over to Betty and swung it back and forth in front of her face. Betty swiped at the bag and yelled at Bonita to get the bag out of her face. Bonita laughed and tossed it on the floor near the garbage can.

"Damn you's a nasty bitch!" Betty exclaimed as she eyed her sister up and down.

"Please don't start no shit today, Betty." Bonita said walking out of her sister's line of vision.

"Why must you always think that every time I have anything to say to you that you don't like, that I'm starting something?"

"Because you do!" Bonita shot back defensively. She continued, "For real, you know you don't have to bring your ass over here right?" Bonita stole a glance at the clock on the wall. She had to get Betty out of there before Frog came back.

"Trust and believe, I am aware of that, but you're my one and only sister and I will make the sacrifice. Besides, you don't have a car to come see me so it's my duty to come check on you. We need to talk about your daughter. Something isn't right with the relationship between you both. "

"Ain't nothing wrong with me, as you can see I'm fine. And as far as Cherry's concerned, I'm sure she's happy as a fucking clam now that she's living with you." Bonita snapped.

"Why are you always so damn mean, Bonita? Or is it all them drugs up in your system that got you thinking and acting crazy and shit? All I'm trying to do is be a good sister to you and a good aunt to my niece.

"What the fuck ever, Ms. Holier than thou! You always thought you and your hot ass daughter were above me and Cherry." Bonita bellowed.

Betty jumped up off the couch and damn near fell over some shoes. She quickly regained her balance and pointed her finger at Bonita. "How the fuck you gonna stand there and say some shit like that out of your mouth? I have never thought I was above you. And don't put Aniya anywhere in this shit. She loves Cherry like a sister and you know this. Look around you, Bonita." She paused. "Look at this mess!" She pointed down at her feet and around the apartment. "See this is what I'm talking about, this kinda shit. How did you even let my niece live in such conditions? And you, Bonita, you look thinner than the last time that I saw you. Your face looks sunken and you've got all kind of marks on it. And is another one of your teeth missing from your head?" Betty pointed to her face.

"Yeah, my tooth fell out so what? Your teeth don't last forever anyway!" Bonita retorted.

Betty got closer to her sister and snatched Bonita's face in her hands. "When are you going to stop using?"

Bonita moved out of her sister's grip and turned her back to Betty. The air hung thick with a mute silence.

Betty softened her voice. "Bonita, you know I love you dearly and I don't want to see anything happen to you or Cherry. You two are the only family I have. Why don't you let me call the rehab center and get you started? You have a daughter that needs you. And you just can't keep doing drugs and think that it's not affecting you or Cherry. Don't you think about your daughter?"

Bonita cringed at the sound of hearing Cherry's name. She was beating herself up over what took place between herself and her only child. But in a defensive mode, Bonita snapped her head back around and got up in her sister's face. "Listen, Betty, maybe I like getting high. And it's my got damn business anyway. I don't see you over here paying any bills or putting any money in my damn pocket!" Bonita yelled.

"What the hell did you just come out your mouth and say!? You know damn well, that's a lie. I gave you money just last month for your fucking rent! Did you forget that? Oh, yeah, you spent the fucking money and I had to come outta pocket again to make sure your dumb ass didn't get put out on the street. That's why I paid the money directly to your slumlord. And then you had the nerve to get mad. And now you got the fucking nerve to be standing here throwing that bullshit in my face. Bonita, you're pathetic. Get it together before you find yourself on skid row and your daughter turns her back on you forever. And speaking of your daughter, what kind of shit do you have her in?" Betty asked.

"Ain't nothing happen with Cherry. I would lay down and die first before I let anything happen to her. Betty, I don't need your help."

"Bitch, you need my help. Look at you! You don't even look like my sister. Back in the day you were one of the baddest chicks on this side of town. You had a body that all the girls were so jealous of. Shit, we used to have to beat bitches down because their men were always openly gawking at you. Look at you now, Bonita, you look like poor black trash!"

Bonita and Betty were a year apart. Betty was the oldest. She was a petite woman with dark flawless skin, a wide nose, thin lips and small hips. She worked at a law firm as a paralegal. Bonita was the street-smart sibling. She had the body of a stripper, which included her thick hips and phat ass. She had a little waist and thin soft arms. But years of drug abuse sent Bonita on a downward spiral mentally and physically. She no longer was the bombshell Diva she used to be. She had lost most of her hair so she cut if all off exposing her lopsided head. Bonita couldn't seduce a dog looking like she did.

"Betty, get off my back and leave me alone!" Bonita barked.

Betty sighed heavily and gazed back at her sister. She knew she was fighting a losing battle. Bonita was in denial about her appearance and her drug habit, and she definitely wasn't talking about what happened between her and Cherry.

Betty threw her hands in the air. "Okay, whatever the hell you want. I ain't saying shit else then. It's your damn life but you just better know this, I am the one taking care of Cherry now because of your incompetence as a mother. Anytime, your own child draws a knife on you and attacks you, then you and your child both need help!"

She continued with her warning, "Now, I don't know what the hell happened in this motherfucker but I know one thing for sure, you are the cause of what has turned your daughter's world upside down. One way or the other, I'ma find out what has transpired up in this bitch!" Betty threatened as Bonita swung around to face her sister.

"If you don't want Cherry's life to be put into danger, you will stay the fuck out of our business. Now, I ain't gonna tell your nosy ass again Betty, on our mother's head, you need to leave the situation between me and my daughter alone. And for God's sakes, don't be running your mouth to anybody else about us either. That's means, stay the fuck outta your preacher's office telling him your business and shit. That doubled tongued motherfucker can't fix one got damn thing. I've seen him down on Baltimore Street running in a peep show. Ain't his sanctified holy ass married with kids?" Bonita emphasized again. "Just let this fucking be for all our sakes. I ain't gonna tell you that shit no more!"

With nothing else to say, Betty and Bonita stared at each other for a moment before Betty turned on her Jimmy Choo pumps and walked out the door slamming it behind her.

As she raced down the steps, she bumped into a skinny young man. His clothes were three sizes too big for him. His hair was matted to his head and he smelled. Just as Betty got to the bottom of the steps, she heard a door open and then recognized the voice speaking to the haggard man as her sister's. Instantly, Betty turned and started back up the steps but was stopped midway when her phone went off. She retrieved her phone and saw Cherry's number on the screen. She looked back up at her sister's door and then at the phone still ringing in her hand. She answered Cherry's call.

With tears bigger than heavy raindrops, Betty walked back down the stairs to her car. While she talked to Cherry, Betty couldn't help but wonder about her sister's life. Would she even be alive in six months? Betty would have to intervene somehow, someway to get her sister back on the right path if her sister were to stay alive and patch up her relationship with her only daughter.

REUNITED AND IT FEELS SO GOOD

Lukie and Tommie sat on the couch playing the newest Madden football video game as Aniya and Cherry fixed dinner. Aniya checked the steaks while Cherry made the salads. Cherry was still somewhat peeved at her cousin for calling Lukie over and wasn't ready to be interrogated by him.

"Cherry, don't be pissed girl. You know that boy loves you and he needed to see you. And I was tired of being asked questions that only you can answer. So pick your lip up off the damn counter and grab the food so we can eat." Aniya said.

With trays in hand piled high with steaks, potatoes and salad, the girls headed towards the dining area.

"Stop, look at me, Cherry!" Aniya willed. Cherry looked at her cousin. "Okay, give me the biggest smile you can. Come on, cuz. I know you're secretly loving the fact that your man is here. So thank me with a smile." Aniya beamed.

Cherry shook her head in defiance, as a huge beautiful smile crept across her flawless face.

"Now that's a good look! Come on, boo, it's time to eat and after that I'm going to my bedroom to play with Tommie's gun." she laughed.

After dinner, Aniya and Tommie retreated to her bedroom leaving Lukie and Aniya alone. Lukie leaned forward on the couch and looked over at his beautiful Cherry. He loved her with all his heart. Never had he let another girl get inside his mind like this, especially if he hadn't hit the skins. He moved close so he could kiss her sweet lips. Cherry kissed her man back with love and passion. When they broke the kiss, Lukie pulled Cherry into his arms. He wasn't going to pressure her about anything right now. He was just happy to see her after being denied for a week. They channel surfed and discussed several movie options but both agreed that was not what they were in the mood for.

Lukie suggested they go out for some fresh air. "Why not take a ride and get out for a little while?"

Cherry knew she was safe with Lukie so she agreed. But first she grabbed her purse.

"You don't need a purse, babe. Come on." Lukie coaxed.

"I don't go anywhere with out my purse. It has my ID and my make up. I always need my lip gloss, Lukie." Cherry laughed.

"I'll be in the car waiting."

Cherry went to the bedroom and could hear Aniya's moans and groans coming through the door. She softly opened it and crept over to the closet where her purse was hanging on the door handle. She put her hand up to her face to block her view of the couple in sexual bliss. She walked past the mirror and froze when she saw Aniya's legs wrapped around Tommie's legs as he grunted with each thrust of his dick in Aniya's wet pussy. She watched momentarily, caught up in their lovemaking.

Aniya was enjoying every minute of Tommie fucking her. Her squeals and moans said so. Aniya's moans were increasing in volume. Cherry watched as Tommie began to move faster inside of Aniya. Both of them were grunting and suddenly Aniya let out a scream.

"I'm cumming. I'm cumming."

Cherry watched her cousin clutch the back of Tommie's back like a vise grip. Her body began to shudder as she gave in to a wave of orgasmic pleasure. Tommie continued with his strokes to get his. Aniya sensing someone was in the room cocked her head over Tommie's shoulder and waved frantically at her cousin to leave. Cherry turned her head away from Aniya as she crept back across the floor and out the room with purse in hand.

Cherry got in the car and stared out the window. Lukie's thought immediately went into overdrive. *Damn, we ain't even out the gate and she's zoning again.* "Cherry, you okay?" he asked.

Seeing her cousin and Tommie made her feel warm all over. "Yep, let's drive. I'm ready to go for a ride." She smiled at Lukie. He turned the key and several minutes later they were on I-95 headed towards Washington DC. Before long, they found themselves at Hains Point. They parked and got out. Cherry remembered there was a famous statue in the park and wanted to see it.

"If you're talking about the man coming out of the ground, they moved him over to the National Harbor, babe." Lukie said.

"Yep, that's him. It's called, *The Awakening*." Cherry acknowledged.

"Well his ass ain't here no more. The artist awakened it and sold it to the Gaylord Hotel."

"Awww, damn, I wanted to see it." Cherry pouted.

"We can drive over there if you want."

"No, it's cool. We're here now."

She looped her hand in Lukie's as they strolled hand and hand around the park. They found a secluded spot under a tree. Lukie leaned back against the tree with Cherry between his legs as they stared at the water. He had to concentrate hard to keep his dick from growing on her back. He wanted Cherry so bad. They small talked for several minutes about nothing. Lukie had been planting little kisses on the back of Cherry's neck. Cherry turned around to face Lukie and kissed him. Before she knew what was happening, she was on the ground with Lukie on top of her looking into her eyes. He stroked the sides of her face and pecked her softly on the lips.

"Cherry, you know you're the only thing that makes me weak. You're like my kryptonite."

"You crazy, boy!" she laughed.

No words were said between them as Lukie and Cherry looked deeply into each other's eyes. Cherry could feel Lukie's heart racing in his chest and Lukie could feel Cherry's soft erratic breathing under his chin. Cherry wrapped her arms around Lukie and hugged him tightly.

"I love you, Lukie." Again, the kissing session started and Cherry began to feel a sense of longing within her body.

A low moan escaped her throat as they kissed. Cherry didn't know what was going on with her body or her senses because everything seemed to be at a heightened level. Lukie was stunned when he felt Cherry grinding herself against him. He ran his hands across Cherry's breast and heard another moan escape her mouth. He broke the kiss and slowly unbuttoned her shirt. He pushed up her bra and exposed her beautiful firm mounds. Cherry's nipples were hard as peaks from excitement and the cool night breeze that wafted across them caused them to stand up taller.

Lukie lowered his hungry mouth over her left breast and gently slid his wet tongue over the hard nipple. He massaged her other breast at the same time. Cherry's moans were louder now. Lukie slid his tongue down the middle of her stomach leaving a wet trail of where he had been. He gently undid Cherry's pants and slid them down. He looked to see if she was zoning but she had her eyes closed in anticipation of his next move. He slipped his forefinger down her panties and slowly fingered her clitoris. Cherry tensed up and Lukie stopped.

"Cherry, let me love you." He said. "Please."

Cherry slowly nodded in agreement and Lukie slid back down to her panties. He pulled them off along with her pants. He took off his blue jean jacket and placed it under Cherry's ass. He then parted her legs and opened her lips. He placed his face between her legs and pressed his tongue on her clitoris. She shuddered. He slowly licked Cherry like an ice cream cone. He grabbed her legs firmly as she had begun to back away from his tongue. After several minutes of licking and fingering her pussy, Cherry was fucking Lukie's face like a wild woman. She didn't know what was going on but she couldn't get enough of what Lukie was doing to her. Her head thrashed from side to side and she grabbed Lukie by the back of his head and pushed his face further into her pussy.

Lukie's dick was hard enough to saw the tree that they were under in half. He stopped giving Cherry head long enough to unzip his pants and pull his boxers down and off of one leg. He gently lay back down on top of Cherry. She parted her legs. Lukie kissed her deeply as he placed his dick at the opening of her pussy. He could feel Cherry's heavy breathing. He kept his eyes on Cherry's as he penetrated her pussy. Little by little he pushed his heavy filled dick in her wetness. When he pushed the last time, both he and Cherry let out a long moan as they became joined as one. Instinctively, Cherry wrapped her legs around Lukie's and moved in a rhythm that she had no control over.

Cherry clung to Lukie like he was her lifesaver. Something was happening deep within her body and Cherry didn't know how to contain it. She only knew of one thing, she had to get to whatever it was that was making her go crazy.

"Lukie.....ummm, Lukie." Cherry hoarsely whispered in the air.

"You feel so good, Cherry!" Lukie had never felt pussy this tight and he wanted to climb inside of it. He stroked Cherry with soft then hard strokes sending her into an ecstasy she'd never experienced. Cherry arched her back to give Lukie more access to her world. He stroked her faster and harder. Unexpectedly, Cherry screeched.

"Yes, Lukie, right there, right there. Don't stop!" Lukie had found her G-spot.

Cherry was throwing her pussy back on Lukie's dick like it was a catcher's mitt. Cherry was starting to feel strange. With every stroke of his dick inside her pussy she was taken to another level of pleasure. Suddenly Cherry's legs tightened around Lukie's and she grabbed his back with new power as Lukie's name pierced through the night air when it escaped her mouth. Cherry's body shuddered violently as an orgasm burst between her legs so hard, Cherry briefly passed out. Lukie's dick continued to involuntarily jump and spit out cum inside of Cherry's sweet, tight, sticky pussy as he gasped for air. Lukie had never cum that hard before in his life.

Cherry threw her arms around Lukie and said, "I'm yours forever."

LIGHTS, CAMERA, ACTION

Stic tapped Trailer Trash on the shoulder. She looked up at him with small bloodshot eyes. He bent down and whispered in her ear. He stepped back as she scooted her chair away from the table and followed him into the next room. "Close the door and get ready," he told her.

Trailer Trash closed the door and undressed completely. Stic walked over to where she stood and stroked her chin. He lifted her head in his hands. "You gonna give me a fucking show that is a stellar performance right, Trailer Trash?"

"Of course." She stood there with a blank look on her face.

He snatched her face hard and peered down into it. "This is costing me a lot today, so I'ma need you to get your mind right and for you to do your fucking job. You hear me, girl?"

She nodded slowly. "If I do a good job, can I go back out there?" she asked like a lifeless five-year old.

"Sure, baby, as a matter of fact, I'll have my chemist mix you a batch of your own shit. How's that? Daddy just wants you to perform like your getting an Oscar okay?" Stic replied.

"I'm not going to let you down."

Moments later, several people walked into the room. They began setting up camera equipment and forty minutes later everything was in place.

"Come on, Trailer, we're ready."

"Here I come."

Trailer waited for instructions on her part in the movie. "Sit on the couch and masturbate for the camera. We're waiting on the star of the show to get ready." Stic advised. He was still coaching her when his phone rang. He answered it and closed it shut. Moments later the star trotted in.

"Now that's what the fuck I'm talkin' 'bout. Shit…lets get this show on the road." Stick clapped his hands together. "Skibop, you did good!" He said to his Lieutenant.

"Thanks, man."

Everyone in the room took their places. Skibop motioned for the star of the show to come over to the couch where Trailer Trash was waiting. Eager to get it over, she got on all fours in a doggy style position as she waited for the star to take his place.

"No, Trailer Trash you need to make him want you. His dick is no different than mine. Do him just like you would do me, baby." Stic suggested.

Trailer Trash crawled over to the star and got underneath his girth. She ran her hand over his balls and watched in horror and excitement at the huge dick that protruded from pink skin and large sack of balls. Immediately her mouth watered at trying this new dick. She opened her mouth and tried to take in the huge dick. It was massive in size. She managed to get just the tip of in her mouth when the pony started bucking. It was trying to fuck Trailer Trash's mouth but she could not accommodate his size.

The camera crew was excited about video taping Trailer Trash giving head to the pony. They didn't want to miss any footage of film as they panned back and forth with the camera and the lighting gear. The horse was overly excited as it tried to ram its thick long dick down her throat. Trailer Trash tried to stop the horse's dick from going into her mouth any further for fear of choking but just as she was about to push herself away, the pony slammed his dick in her mouth so hard, it snapped her head back onto the bed. She furiously began waving her hands at the camera trying to get their attention.

"Cut!" The director yelled. "And get the horse."

The horse was lead back to the side and Trailer Trash was able to recover. The director of the movie went over to Trailer and asked, “Are you okay?”

“I think.”

“I need you over here now.” He pointed to another side of the set. “We are going to try something else.”

As he was getting ready to shoot, Stic said, “Wait a minute.” He looked at Skibop. “Get that package in the other room. I want to make sure Trailer Trash is good and ready.”

Skibop returned with a tray with a pipe on it. He snatched Trailer Trash by the arm and sat her up on the couch. “Here, bitch, take your medicine.”

She greedily snatched the pipe and sprinkled the powder that was in the spoon over top of some tobacco. She lit the pipe and pulled heavily. The smoke disappeared into the pipe and her lungs filled with the drug. She exhaled and was immediately lifted. Skibop went to get up when Trailer Trash snatched him by the arm.

“Damn, bitch, wait a minute, I’ma let your greedy ass have another hit.” Skibop prepared another hit and let Trailer Trash suck on the pipe once more. Now she was in her childlike zombie state.

“She’s ready. Let’s do this! This camera crew is costing me a fucking grip.” Stic said.

“Bring the horse back over here and position him!” the director said.

“Trailer, I want you to fuck the shit out that horse dick. You hear me, bitch. Fuck the shit out of that dick.”

Trailer Trash looked up at Stic and a half smile eased over her face. Skibop brought the pony back to the middle of the room.

“Get on all fours and let the Star of the Show do what the fuck he knows how to do. Fuck that flat ass.” He laughed.

Trailer Trash got on all fours and Skibop brought the pony to the back of Trailer Trash’s waiting ass. The pony instinctively, ready to mate, humped the air. Trailer Trash, reached behind her and grabbed a hold of the huge dick. She slowly guided it to her pussy. The pony didn’t need any more coaching, as it found her pussy hole and slammed itself into her as far as it could go. Trailer Trash let out a wail of a cry as the pony fucked her fast and deep.

The pony held on to her back like a man, as it slammed its long, thick dick into her pussy. Trailer Trash's cries of pain soon gave way to pleasure as she closed her eyes and didn't move. She let the pony have its way with her. She began to masturbate her clitoris while the Star of the Show fucked her like a man. About eight minutes into the fuck fest, Trailer Trash let out another wail of passion as an orgasm escaped her pussy. The Star of the Show bucked several more times and pulled out of Trailer Trash's wetness.

His huge red dick squirted horse cum all over the back of Trailer Trash's ass. The camera crew went wild about the footage they taped and was already talking about the edits. Skibop and several others watched the scene with disgust and a deep disrespect of Trailer Trash. They couldn't believe a woman would stoop so low, as to fuck an animal just for a drug.

"Damn, if getting a woman to do something like that, is that easy," Skibop said to himself, "I might have to investigate the use of Mind Bend on one of my hoes."

Stic watched the entire episode with one thing on his mind, how to expand his distribution area of Mind Bend. After the pony was lead out of the room, the camera crew packed up their gear and left. Trailer Trash sat on the side of the couch butt naked looking into space. She didn't say a word after her sexual performance was over.

Stic went into the bathroom and came back with a towel. He threw it at her. "Wrap your skank as up. I ain't tryin' to see your nasty ass."

She hid herself in the towel and continued to space out. "Did you like getting fucked by the horse?" he asked.

"No, I didn't like that, daddy." She replied.

"Well I couldn't tell the difference the way you was screaming and cumming all over the horse's dick." Trailer Trash didn't say anything as she looked at the wall behind Stic. "Yeah, I know you liked it. It's cool, baby. Daddy ain't gonna spank your ass tonight. I'll be by later to check on ya'll. But be happy, you did your first porn movie with a horse as opposed to your usual…dogs."

"Did I do good? Just how you liked?"

"Trailer, that shit was a turn on as well as just plain nasty. But your daddy's number one trick and your movies bring in big bucks. Go on and get the hell outta of here. I'll see your ass later."

While they spoke, Dominitra was in the dressing room cleaning it up. He witnessed the scene with Trailer Trash and the horse and shook his head in pity. He didn't understand how Trailer did the things she did and let Stic use and abuse her that way. He felt sorry for her. She was a slave to Stic and that drug. There was nothing that he could do anyway to help her. She was Stic's property and Stic was the head nigga in charge. To cross him meant death and he loved his life too much to put it on the line for any of the porn stars on the compound.

He finished picking up the clothes and thought about when he was going to be called back to Stic's bedroom for some sweet lovemaking. It was the only thing on his mind.

A RE-NIGGA

Trailer Trash was back to her room. She wasn't sure what she'd done but knew it was something that she would not have done if she wasn't high. She crawled into her bed and hugged the worn out pillow. The case on the pillow was long overdue for a change as well as her sheets. But Trailer Trash didn't care. She didn't even care about washing her ass. All she wanted was more Mind Bend. The opening of another door in the hallway caused her to put the pillow over her head and sink further into the bed. Voices filled with laughter and chatter rushed noisily in the outer room.

"Girl, did you see that sorry ass trick that I had? He wasn't about shit! First of all, I couldn't find his dick because it was no bigger than my thumb and then his sorry ass wanted to negotiate the damn prices. I know damn well, Big Blue told him exactly how much it was to get fucked. He agreed to it. So I took his ass in the room, worked his little dick off and then asked for payment. Girl, why he try to say he didn't have all the money?"

"Oh my Gawd, Carnival. Was that your John I heard screaming like that?" Tawni asked laughing.

"Yeah, girl. You know I couldn't let that mothafucka leave without paying me what the fuck he owed. Girl, when he reached for his pants, I went under the mattress and pulled out my baton. I told that stupid mothafucka he was going to pay me. If he didn't, he had a choice of either me or Big Blue beating his ass for reneging. He saw Big Blue so he opted for me instead."

"Carnival, did you whoop that ass?" Tawni asked as she high fived Carnival.

"Did I? I made that mothafucka give me my money first and then I told his ass he could either lay down across the bed or stand. Either way, I was delivering that ass a beating. I hit the button for Big Blue and he came in and stood guard at the door. And you know Blue always gets a kick outta seeing a grown man get his ass beat like a child and especially by my little ass!" Carnival laughed.

"Yeah, that shit makes his face light up like a Christmas tree. So which did you use?" Tawni asked.

"I grabbed the college board. You know the one with the holes in it. I snatched that bitch up and swung it like a tennis racket right across that motherfucka's ass. Girl, he screamed like a bitch and took off running, right into Big Blue. Blue pushed his ass down on the bed and held him while I beat him with my paddle like a bad little boy.

"He was screaming so hard, he passed the fuck out. Big Blue pulled him off the bed and threw him and his tent for pants out the door. His ass won't be able to sit down for the next week. And I know he ain't gonna short another hoe as long as he lives." Carnival said laughing so hard she choked.

"Girl, you a mess!" Tawni replied.

"You know Stic don't play that shit. Besides Stic has been going up side my head lately. I don't know what's crawled up his ass, but I ain't taking no chances with him. Sometimes, I wonder if he on that shit he be feeding Trailer."

"Yeah, I feel you on that shit, Carnival. He's been on my ass too. Shit, I can't make mothafuckas fuck me. And my movies ain't selling as fast as they used to. I told Stic the recession's bad. Men ain't spending money like that! But of course, Stic says that I ain't putting my all into it, that I need a new way to approach my Johns and a devise a marketing strategy. He kills me talking all collegiate and shit." Tawni said.

"Tawni, it's all good. We make it do what it gotta do when it gotta do it. Don't worry about that shit now. Let's see what new gear we got for this next movie." Carnival said dumping the bags that she was carrying on the couch.

Both girls began going through the new clothes they bought when Carnival noticed Trailer Trash walking towards them. Carnival tapped Tawni on the arm and nodded her head toward Trailer Trash. Tawni rolled her eyes and continued looking at the clothes.

Carnival decided to check on Trailer Trash. She walked over to the chair where Trailer Trash was sitting and perched herself on the arm. Carnival gently tapped Trailer Trash on the shoulder. "Trailer, you okay girl? Did you have to work today?"

Trailer scooted as close to the other side of the chair as she could get.

"Trailer, I'm just checking on a bitch to make sure you good." Carnival said standing up. Trailer locked eyes with Carnival briefly before returning her stare back to her hands. Carnival shrugged her shoulders and walked back over to the couch, where Tawni was trying on a tight multi-color sequenced dress. Carnival burst out laughing.

"Bitch, what's so funny? I know you ain't laughing at my dress. Shit this right here cost me $29.99." She said twirling around in the ill-fitting dress.

"Girl, it looks like it cost $29.99. Where in the hell did you ever find a fuckin' multicolor sequenced dress? What the hell?"

"Girl, stop hating. You just jealous. I look good in this shit. Wait 'till I put this on for one of the roles I got coming up."

"No, please don't put that shit on, not even for Halloween. Girl, take that ridiculous thang back to where you bought it and slap the sales clerk for even selling you that shit." Carnival roared with laughter as if she didn't have a care in the world.

Trailer Trash sat quietly, wishing she could feel as happy as they did. Instead, all she felt was shame.

CAT FIGHT

"What the fuck is going on up in this bitch, Dominitra? Huh?" Stic yelled, with an attitude.

Dominitra ran across the room. "Oh lawd, I don't know. I was in Carnival's room getting her ready for her shoot, when we heard a loud commotion. When I came out, I saw Trailer Trash running down the hall like she lost her ever loving mind!"

"And didn't nobody stop that bitch to see what's wrong with her crazy ass?" Stic questioned.

"Like I said, I was in here beating Ms. Carnival's face. What you need to do with that fish is lock her in a damn rubber room. She running around here scaring the shit out of everybody cause she ain't high no more. Baby, you need to do something with that!" Dominitra replied. "I can't be everywhere all the time."

Stic stood in the hallway of his compound. He was sick of Trailer Trash going crazy when she couldn't get high. "Look, Dominitra find that crazy bitch and settle her down. You hear me?!" Stic's nose flared as he hollered at Dominitra.

"I'm on it, Stic."

"I'm going to the house. I don't expect to hear anymore shit coming from the pound. Handle these bitches, Dominitra. That's what you paid to do. I don't want to have to come back down this way!" Stic stormed out of the door and faded into the night.

Dominitra was beside himself. He didn't know if he could handle Trailer Trash right now. Dominitra tried talking to Trailer Trash when she came back from the shoot but she was withdrawn and would not talk to anybody. Dominitra shook his head as he went back to Carnival to finish her makeup. Today, he was in full drag himself.

"Why doesn't Stic just get rid of that white girl? It ain't like he needs her and shit. He constantly has to keep her ass high as a jet just to get her to do anything." Carnival snipped.

"He keeps her because she does all kinds of shit that neither you or Tawni's ghetto ass will do." He laughed. "Well, do of your own free will anyway." Dominitra replied. "Close your eyes so I can put your shadow on." Dominitra continued to make up Carnival's face when Tawni came in bursting through the door. Dominitra immediately turned his back to Tawni as he continued to apply eye shadow to Carnvial's lids.

"Dominitra, I need to take a dress back to the store so when you're done with Carnival, we need to go." Tawni said popping gum and ghetto standing. Dominitra continued Carnival's makeup job. "Dominitra, I know you hear me talking to you. I said…"

"I heard what you said, tramp!" He said whisking around to look at Tawni. Dominitra threw his hands on his hips. "Bitch, don't come up in here demanding shit. You ask me if I mind taking your ghetto ass back into town. Like you got manners." He snapped his fingers and rolled his eyes at Tawni.

"Don't start the dramatics, Dom. All I want is for you to take me back to the store to exchange a dress for another one. I'm scheduled for a shoot tomorrow. Can you do that for me?"

"Say please, bitch!"

"Okay, Dominitra." Tawni said with her teeth clenched. "Can you please take me into town?"

Dominitra rolled his neck. "I'll think about it. You always acting all stank and shit with yours. You make doing anything for you hard. Shit, just to like you takes all my strength."

"Faggot, please, I'm not asking your punk ass to like me. I really don't give a shit if you do or not cause the only one giving me anything up in here is Stic. My alliance is to him, not you. All you supposed to do is take care of us like the faggotty dramatic ass mother hen that you are."

"You sound ridiculous."

"It's true. Your job is to make sure we have what we need, when we need it. Now do I have to pick up the line to Stic and complain that I ain't getting what I need?" She conjured. "It's your choice."

Carnival watched the chewing gum fly out of Tawni's mouth as Dominitra snatched Tawni by her hairweave and began to shake her head. Tawni was caught off guard by Dominitra's attack and could do nothing but claw at Dominitra's hands. Suddenly Tawni felt her legs give from under her, as Dominitra pushed her back over top of a chair. Tawni fell to the floor and Dominitra took control and pummeled Tawni's head against the bottom of the make-up chair.

Big Blue just opened the door and was greeted by the fight. He watched the cat fight for a minute to see who was winning. Clearly, the chair was winning because Dominitra was wearing Tawni's head out with it. Carnival stepped in and tried to pull Dominitra off of Tawni. That was Big Blue's queue. With one scoop, he picked up a screaming Tawni in his arms. Dominitra scrambled back to his feet before she got up in Tawni's face.

"Whore, you better be glad that all I did was snatch that weave off your head." He said throwing patches of weave in Tawni's face. "Be lucky!"

"I'm going to kill you!"

"Blue, take that bitch outta here right now before I forget that I am a lady today and whoop her ass like the man that I truly am!"

Blue took a still screaming Tawni out the door. Carnival picked Dominitra's wig up and handed it to him. Carnival shook her head as she sat back in the make-up chair, while Dominitra finished the job. "Don't say shit about it. Just let me finish you so I can go have a damn drink. That little girl got me fucked up!"

Carnival didn't part her mouth to say shit. She was just happy that Stic wasn't called back down to the compound. Because if he was, she wasn't sure what he would have done or who might have been left standing alive.

STORY TIME

Dominitra picked up the phone on the second ring. He put his jeans, tank top and shoes on and made his way out the door. An hour later he lay in the bed next to Stic. They had just finished a fuck session that had him wheeling in contented sexual glory.

Stic swung his feet over the bed and pushed them into his leather slippers. He donned his plush robe and went to the wet bar on the other side of his huge bedroom and poured a drink. Dominitra was lying in the bed with a huge smile on his face. He could still smell their sex in between the sheets.

Stic sat down in one of the high back winged chairs in the seating area of his bedroom. He called for Dominitra to join him. He sat across from Stic with a glass of wine. Stic swirled the ice in his glass, looked at the contents of the brown liquid and then took a gulp. "Another porn star will be joining us soon. She's very special to me so I want her on the other side of the compound away from the other girls. I got special plans for this one, Dominitra. So get the room set up for her. I also have a construction crew coming to build me a few things in the room next to where she will be residing. Make sure the crew do their jobs and get the fuck out. They shouldn't be there more than two days. Anything after that, you let me know." Stic said in between sips of his drink.

Just what the fuck I need, another fish tail up in here! Dominitra thought to himself.

"When is she coming?" He asked.

"When the fuck she gets here! Don't you worry about her time of arrival! Like a thief in the night, she'll be here. Just get shit done!" Stic scolded.

"Stic, I'm not trying to upset you. Why you always get so tense with me? You know I'm just looking out for you, boo." Dominitra said.

Stic cringed at being called boo by Damon.

"Look, Damon," he said, calling him by his government name, "just be ready. You can go on back to the Pound now. I got shit to do."

Dominitra downed his wine and angrily set the glass down on the wet bar counter. He quickly put on his clothes. Stic turned the T.V. on to Sports Center, while Dominitra stood in front of him.

Stic gazed up at him. "What, Da?"

"Can I get some more love before I leave?" He asked with his arms outstretched, to receive a hug from Stic.

"Da, I got what I needed, so all I want you to do now is leave. I told you I got shit to do anyway. Now move, you blocking my view." He pushed Dominitra to the right.

Not to be put off, Dominitra knelt down on the side of the chair. His heart was breaking. He had to ask. "Stic, what happened to us? There was a time when you couldn't wait to be with me. We were somewhat of a couple. But you began to drift away after you started this movie business."

Stic looked intently at him. "This movie business is what keeps your black ass with a job."

Dominitra continued, unfazed by Stic's comment. "Stic, the only reason I agreed to take the job you offered me as the "woman" of the house, was because I'm crazy about you. I thought you felt the same way about me. But somewhere that changed." He softly said.

Stic was tired of hearing Dominitra's voice; let alone what was coming out of his mouth. He abruptly stood up. He had to keep him in check, but he also had to keep him under his thumb. He chose to play on his heart.

"Da, I'm sorry if I haven't been as attentive as I was. You know I'm running mad shit in here and out there. You're gonna have to man up and roll with the punches on this one. I got love for you." Stic said pounding his chest with his fist. Sensing this eased his mind he continued to poison it. "When I'm done with a few things, maybe we'll go back to California and stay a few days at that beach house that you liked so much." Stic lied.

Stic wanted to throw up at his own words. Dominitra was grinning from ear to ear now. He accepted Stic's lies. He hugged Stic and said, "I love you."

Stic kept his hand from taking the glass that was in it and crashing it across Dominitra's skull. Instead he stood stiff as a board while being hugged. He got what he wanted from Dominitra and that was sexual relief. Now all he wanted was for him to get the fuck out of his room and back to the compound with the rest of the nasty bitches.

"D, go on back to the pound and I'll get with you later about what we talked about and about taking you away."

"I'm on it, Stic. You can count on me." Dominitra's happy ass practically skipped out the door.

When he left, Stic wrenched in his stomach and ran to the bathroom to relieve the contents of it. "The cost of doing business is higher than I thought."

BROKEN CHERRY

Cherry, Aniya, Tommie and Lukie were sitting in *Johnny Rockets* at Arundel Mills Mall, talking about what to do for Cherry's upcoming birthday which was the following Friday. Aniya noticed Lukie and Cherry couldn't keep their hands off one another and that they were smiling and giggling like they were in the sixth grade.

Aniya tapped Tommie on the arm. "Tommie, you thinking' what I'm thinking?" she asked.

"Hell yeah, they finally did the wild thang. Look at Lukie smiling all hard and shit and Cherry ain't shut her mouth since we got together."

"Yeah, last night she came in the room to get her purse and saw us getting down." Aniya laughed. "Maybe she was inspired.'

"What you mean she saw us?" Tommie asked with a puzzled look across his face.

"Just what I said, she came in to get her purse. I caught her ass watching you throw the dick. That may have been all she needed to see to go back out there and jump on Lukie's shit. Put it this way, whatever happened when those two went out last night, didn't bring back the same two people. Somewhere they stopped and got broke the fuck off." Aniya affirmed. "And I'm damn sure gonna make Cherry give me every detail about it too. We ain't leaving no stone unturned. You need to check your boy and make sure he didn't hurt Cherry."

"What the hell you mean hurt her? He ain't no rapist or murderer or nothing like that." Tommie said in defense of his boy.

Aniya pulled Tommie closer to her and whispered, "Cherry was never touched by any man. So if Lukie got it, he got a virgin pussy."

Tommie's face lit up. "You fucking kidding me right? Come on, Cherry ain't no virgin, Niya!" Tommie chided.

"Tommie, if I tell you something about me and my cousin, you can play the lottery on that. You know I know just about everything about her. And I do know that Cherry is a virgin or was a virgin until last night with Lukie."

"Well from the looks of it, her Cherry has been popped." Tommie whispered back.

"What the hell are you two whispering about over there?" Lukie asked.

"Nothing man, we just waiting on the food." Tommie said grinning like a Chester cat.

Aniya pursed her lips and pointed her finger at Cherry. "So where did you two run off too last night?" Aniya inquired.

"We went for a ride to D.C. at Hains Point to see the "Awakening" statue but it's been moved. So we walked around the park and talked. That's all. We needed to clear some stuff between us." Cherry conceded.

"I bet ya'll cleared some stuff!" Tommie chuckled.

Cherry and Lukie shared eye contact and smiled. They were lost in each other momentarily. The waitress arrived back at the table with a platter of double cheeseburgers along with two steaming platters of cheese fries. They ate, talked and laughed. Cherry was in love even deeper after letting Lukie make love to her. She felt good. She couldn't wait to get Lukie alone again so they could do it again.

She reached her hand up to Lukie's face and whispered something in his ear that caused him to choke on his fries. He snatched Cherry around by the waist and planted a sloppy kiss on her.

"Ewww, get a room damn it! People are eating here." Aniya playfully said.

"Yeah we might have to." Lukie said looking into Cherry's eyes. Cherry's wide smile that creased across each end of her face confirmed for Aniya and Tommie that Lukie had officially broken Cherry's chastity belt.

"Okay break that shit up. You two are getting all mushy and shit. Let's talk about what we gonna do for your birthday, Cherry." Aniya said.

"I'm taking my baby away for the weekend of her birthday. We're gonna chill for the weekend. I already reserved a two bedroom suite for all of us at the Gaylord Resort at the National Harbor." Lukie interjected.

Cherry and Aniya's girly giggles went into overdrive and Tommie and Lukie gave each other a pound. The four continued their rounds of talking, eating burgers and drinking chocolate and banana milkshakes. It was decided that they would hit a few clubs in DC since they would be in the area anyway.

Life was looking up for Cherry, and suddenly things didn't seem so bad.

MIRROR MIRROR

Damon was in his room. He put away his girly alter ego, Dominitra, for the evening. He was visibly upset with the conversation he previously had with Stic. Yet he was hopeful about their relationship. But who was the new bitch that he was bringing in and why? It wasn't like Stic needed money. He was a millionaire several times over. Between his Mind Bend product and his movies, Stic could be on the Fortune 500 list if it was legal.

He just finished putting away what he wore earlier. He already took off his makeup and wig after his fight with Tawni. Besides, he wanted to be ready for Stic's call. Stic didn't like doing Damon in drag all the time. He told Damon he wanted to know what he was fucking. If it was a man then let it be a man. And if it was a woman then it had to be a woman. He didn't play that pretend shit in the bedroom. Outside of the bedroom, Stic called Damon by his drag name when he saw Damon dressed as Dominitra.

Damon knew that Stic had women on the outside of the compound that he was fucking. If Damon had his way, Stic would never fuck another pussy at all. But Stic went both ways and Damon conceded that no matter how hard he tried to please Stic sexually, he couldn't get Stic to completely commit to just him.

Damon sat down at his vanity dresser and looked at himself in the mirror. He was still relatively handsome with a well-kept washboard abdomen. He had beautiful pecan brown skin that he maintained with a cleansing and moisturizing ritual. He had no facial hair and two beautiful dimples sat just below his coco brown eyes. Damon could have gotten any man that he wished but when he took one look at Stic working out at the gym, he fell in love. Now he didn't know how to feel about him.

Damon sighed heavily as he sat down in the gold vanity chair and peered into the Hollywood lit vanity mirror. "Why do you let Stic treat you the way he does? It's clear that he doesn't love you like you love him." He said to his reflection. He waited for an answer and as always, his answer returned void. He put his head down on the vanity and let go of his pent up tears. His pity party was interrupted by a knock at his door.

He quickly wiped his eyes, as the door slightly opened and he heard Trailer Trash whisper if she could come in.

"Come on." He waved her inside.

She looked haggard as she slowly walked over to his bed and sat down. Damon didn't like anyone on his bed and especially the porn queens. He pointed to the chaise lounge and Trailer Trash plopped her ass on it instead. He waited for her to speak.

"Dominitra, did Stic give you anything today for me?" She asked.

He sighed. "No, Trailer. He didn't."

"I feel like I'm going crazy, Dominitra. I don't know how much longer I can do this." She mumbled.

"Do what, Trailer?" He pushed aside his feelings and genuinely gave his attention to her.

He didn't have any problems with Trailer Trash except when she would go crazy because she was crashing from her high. Those times he'd subdue her by damn near knocking her head off.

Trailer softly whimpered. She was melancholy. Dominitra remained silent to let Trailer have her moment. Trailer sniffed heavily and raised her eyes to meet Dominitra's. Trailer's eyes beheld sadness, loneliness and depression. Whatever hopes and ambitions Trailer Trash possessed, were long trampled on and removed by Stic.

Trailer sat quietly within her own thoughts for a minute. She sniffed again and wiped the side of her face with the back of her hands. She slowly brought her hands to rest in her lap. She examined them as if there was something on them.

"These hands were going to be great, Dominitra." She continued, "Do you know I was in one of the most prestigious colleges in America?" She shifted in her seat. "My hands were supposed to be surgeon's hands." She paused and then looked up.

"I didn't know that."

"I should have been standing in an operating room right now saving a life. Instead, I began to party and my grades dropped. And when my grades dropped so did my attitude about school. My parents found out and hit the fucking roof."

"What happened?"

"They of course did what most parents would have done. Cut off my tuition and allowance. So, I just didn't give a fuck anymore." She paused again.

"I'm sorry to hear that, girl. I didn't know you were going to be a doctor."

"It's okay."

"I have to ask, how in the hell did you go from being in an Ivy League college to ending up here turning tricks and fucking everything from rocks to animals?"

Trailer shifted again uneasily on the chaise. She was ashamed of herself and what she had become. She looked up again and answered one word. "Sticory."

"Sticory? How, what happened?" Dominitra asked.

"Stic was all the girls could talk about. White girls, black girls, Asian girls, even a few of those girls that wore those long dresses and covered up from head to toe wanted him. In case you haven't noticed, he is one fine black man." Dominitra cleared his throat and Trailer proceeded.

"He was one of few black men who were in college in the medical field, especially to become a pharmacist. I met Sticory through some mutual friends at a frat party one night. And you know how we party." Trailer laughed.

"Like rock stars?" Dominitra heckled.

"Yeah, like fucking rock stars, man. Anyway, Sticory was at the party. He could have had any of the girls that night but he kept making eye contact with me. Eventually we had a conversation which led way to sex and sex led the way to falling in love." She breathed heavily and averted her eyes back to her hands in her lap.

"He's easy to fall in love with."

"Yes he is." She paused. "Stic came over to my dorm and told me that he was working on some new formula to get a major high on. He said it was still in its early stages. One night, we all went out for drinks and I had one. Before I could finish the drink, I was high as Mount Everest. I couldn't function and Stic ended up taking me home."

"He put something in your drink?" Dominitra asked. He wouldn't be surprised.

"He had to. Because I've drank way more than one glass and never felt like I did that night." She replied.

"Did you ask him about it?"

"Of course I did. But he said that I must have imagined that I only drank one drink. He said I had several. I don't remember that shit though." Another pause, "Stic raped me that night." She confessed. "I never forgot about it."

Dominitra sat up straight. "Stic raped you? Are you sure you weren't dreaming?" He asked.

"He threw me on the bed, took a pair of stockings from his pocket and tied my hands. He pushed my skirt up and tore off my panties. Next thing I felt was his dick tearing my pussy up." She said. "Does that sound like I had to much to drink and didn't remember?" She replied.

In as much as Dominitra loved Stic, he didn't like the fact that he raped someone. He found that to be cowardly, of any man taking a woman's pussy, especially against her will. "Why didn't you tell the police and have his ass locked up? Were you scared of him?"

"No, I wasn't scared. As a matter of fact," Trailer hesitated and then gushed, "I loved every fucking minute of him raping me. I was so turned on that I came several times and he didn't even know it. God, his dick was so big and good. I would have gladly fucked him. He didn't have to rape me. I wanted his dick the moment I laid eyes on him at the party. But he didn't give me a chance to go there."

Dominitra confused over after hearing Trailer Trash's secret. He stared at her in absolute shock until he found his voice to speak. "You're telling me that you liked being raped by Stic? Is that what the fuck you just confessed too?" Dominitra asked, throwing his hands in the air and getting up off the vanity stool.

"I know it's crazy, but it's the truth."

"I can't believe you said that shit. Chile, you are truly special, Trailer Trash. Truly special! Only a bitch like you would like that type of shit. He named you right when he tagged your ass with Trailer Trash." Dominitra spewed.

"I know it's weird but I couldn't help it."

Dominitra went from feeling sorry for Trailer Trash, to wanting to beat her ass. What kind of sick shit was that to be raped by a man and like it? Dominitra didn't want to hear anymore of Trailer's true confessions so she pointed to the door.

"Trailer, do you know how many girls get raped by men and are fucked up behind that shit? For the rest of their lives? You got to go, girl. Right now!"

Trailer's eyes welled up with tears and she exploded into a loud cry. "I knew you wouldn't understand."

Dominitra stomped his foot. "Stop that shit, Trailer. I ain't trying to hear no sobbing right now. I got shit to sob about my damn self. Now stop it!" He hollered.

"Dominitra, please, I need someone to talk to. I told you I'm going crazy. I don't know how much longer I can do this!" Trailer pleaded in between loud gagging sobs. "I don't want to fuck anything or anyone else and I'm tired of Stic filling me up with that damn drug and making me! I want to get the fuck outta of here!" she yelled.

"That's not my problem."

"Please Dominitra, help me! Please just help me!" Trailer Trash wept falling off the chaise lounge and onto her face on the floor.

Dominitra rushed to her side. “Mary Ann, get up, chile. It’s gonna be okay.” Damon softly said, as he helped her back onto the Chaise. This situation called for them to speak to each other using their real names.

“I need help. And I’m asking for yours.”

The soft spot for her returned. Damon sat beside Mary Ann on the lounge and listened to the rest of her story. Mary Ann described how she and Stic had a love-hate relationship while he was in college. She explained that she ended up dropping out because of her financial constraints and her excessive partying. Before Stic graduated, he broke it off with Mary Ann. Devastated, she returned to Baltimore. Her parents were ashamed of her because of her failure in college and their broken dreams of her becoming a surgeon.

After being dejected, Mary Ann took to the streets. One day she happened to run into Aston at a different party. Aston knew Stic. By that time, Stic and Aston had perfected their new drug called, Mind Bend. When Mary Ann saw Stic, her old feelings came back and before long, she hooked up with him again. But this time, he hooked her onto his drug. Mary Ann was moved into the compound and brainwashed to do any and everything to keep the high. Stic put her in his movies and renamed her “Trailer Trash” because she acted just like the name.

After Mary Ann’s mini break down, Damon ushered her to the opening of his door. But before leaving, she turned and faced Damon. Her eyes beseeched Damon as her steely cold fingertips snaked around his wrists. “Damon, I don’t want to die in here. Help me.” Before Damon could respond, she merged into the obscurity of the hallway.

Damon’s heart was gripped by Mary Ann’s visit. She was spiraling down fast and there was no telling what she might do. Still there was nothing that he could do to save her or anyone else in the compound. He walked over to the window and peered out at his reality, a secluded, solitary crazy place called “The Compound.”

Stic sought and found a large piece of land that was deeply hidden within a thickly wooded area. He bought the land and built a fortress. It was surrounded with an electric, barbed-wire ten-foot high fence. Two guard towers that housed the latest in surveillance technology, kept an electronic watch over the land. The equipment was manned by Big Blue.

Sometimes Stic would run through the recorded DVD's, to make sure everything was on point. Every window had bars across it making escape virtually impossible without dynamite or C-4. It was like living in a cage. Even if you did escape, getting out of the exterior of the fenced area was a feat in and of itself. The Compound sat so far away from a main road, that it took fifteen minutes by any mode of transportation to get there.

The Compound had three levels. The first level being the entrance hosted the usual, kitchen, living room, dining room and den. Upstairs were four small bedrooms that had their own baths and two separate bathrooms made up the right side of the Compound. On the left side were two other rooms. One was a large bedroom and the other was one of Stic's private rooms within the Compound. It remained locked and the only person who ever entered was Stic or Dominitra upon request. There was another building to the right of the Compound which was the porn studio. The camera crew was only allowed in this area of the Compound. The studio had its own entrance and driveway.

Looks were deceiving because behind the huge redwood fence that lined the back of the Studio, laid the Compound. The Compound's basement was completely off limits to everyone except Dominitra. This large open arena was Stic's playground of truth. When motherfuckers in the street acted a damn fool, they were brought back to the Compound through a secret entrance and the truth would be known. A large modern Victorian house was built a half a mile down the road from the Compound. Stic spent the majority of his time there, if he wasn't at one of the apartments out in Baltimore or Montgomery counties.

When he was at the Compound, it was usually to check on his moneymakers and to make deals. There was one phone line in

Stic's house; it was a direct line to the Compound. Stic could pick up the line and dial 247. And someone needed to pick the phone up right away. He didn't care who it was, just as long as his call was answered.

One afternoon, Damon remembered coming home from the market to find Carnival cowering in the corner of the living room. She was holding her arm and crying. He approached her.

"Carnival, what's wrong with you, chile? Get up."

"Stic… Stic.." she blubbered.

Damon knew something happened. He put the bags down on the dinette table and reached for Carnival. When Damon pulled on Carnival's arm, she screamed in pain. Shocked at her scream and reaction, he let her go. "Carnival, what the hell happened? Did Stic come down here?" he asked.

"Yes and he beat me." Carnival confessed.

Distressed Damon asked, "Why? What did you do?"

"I didn't hear the phone ringing because I was in the shower and Tawni was with a John."

"Oh God!" Damon gasped. "Let me see how badly you're hurt." He softly took the arm that and inspected it. "Wiggle your fingers!"

Carnival tried but nothing happened. She flinched in severe pain at trying to do the movements. "It won't work."

Damon softly pressed his fingers along Carnival's arm and she winced in pain. "Your arm is broke." He confirmed.

Upon further inspection, Dominitra saw that Carnival had several broken fingers as well. "Damn, Carnival, Stic fucked your arm and hand up badly. Chile, now I got to call Stic and tell him we need the doctor."

From that point on Carnival took her showers with the door open and the phone on the toilet seat. Stic also had some of Baltimore's finest crooked officers on hand. The lure of plentiful cash and additional perks that Stic afforded, made them almost as thuggish as Stic's own crew. At times they forgot who the fuck they were working for, which was.

Stic was well informed in advance on anything that might hinder his operation. He didn't keep any drugs on the premises other than what he brought weekly for his 'Trailer Trash'. A Wells Fargo safe was nestled on the bottom level of the Compound, behind a hidden wall. In the safe was over eight million in cash, passports and several encrypted flash-drives with information on the corrupted police officers. He also kept other devices like the one he kept on a keychain which stayed in his pocket. Dominitra was Stic's confidant as well as his lover. But as Stic's power, money and ambition grew, Stic's interest in being with Damon waned.

The things Stic cared about now were making more money and putting his latest find to work on the screen.

As he considered what was to become of his life, Dominitra suddenly felt nostalgic. He was longing to be free. Free from his bondage of the Compound and free from his love of Stic. He shook his head at the inability to do either. He was sworn to secrecy about the Compound, as were, Tawni, Carnival, Trailer Trash and Big Blue. They all were lured by Stic's money and his promise of fame for the porn stars. Once he had them hooked, he enslaved them and threatened their lives and the lives of their loved ones. Even his crew of Moop, Batman and Skibop were all sworn to keep The Compound a jeweled secret. To cross Stic was certain death. There was another member of Stic's crew who did such a thing. Damon recalled that night and grew worried.

Damon was summoned to the basement of the Compound. Instantly his legs wobbled. He knew what that meant. When he arrived, Skibop and Moop were standing in front of the "Truth". The Truth was a specially made chair, which was bolted to the floor to ensure its stability. The bottom of the chair had a release lever that could be engaged so the back of the chair could be pushed down into a table like position.

The room was soundproofed and was totally washable by a hose just like the one Batman cleaned at the hidden cave. Securely confined to the chair was Gappy. Gappy was a trusted solider in

Stic's underworld army. He knew Stic's rules and knew of Stic's reputation. He had followed every one of the rules and didn't understand why he was now in the Truth chair. He tried his best not to defecate on himself. His nerves were running rampant; he could hear the blood coursing through his veins. Each minute that ticked away made Gappy feel faint. Moop and Skibop anxiously awaited Stic's arrival. Several minutes later Stic appeared in the room.

"Well, well, well. What did the lion drag in today?" No one said a word as everyone knew Stic always said this cliché' before he questioned his victim. Stic stood in front of Gappy before he leaned down in Gappy's face.

"Stic, I don't know what's happening."

"Gappy, my man, I'm only gonna ask you this one time, nigga. If what comes out your mouth doesn't match the information that I have, you gonna have a bad day at the office. Who was you talking too?"

Eyes full of terror and anxiety in his voice, Gappy tried to explain. "Stic,...I don't know what you're talking about, man. Honestly, I don't know why I'm here!"

"Gappy, you gotta have some idea why you're here." Stic taunted.

"Noooo, I don't. Come on, Stic man, what is this about?" A panic-stricken Gappy asked.

"Damn, my nigga, you really don't know why your here? Well how about your mouth wrote a check your ass couldn't cash!" Stic cajoled.

An obtuse look crossed over Gappy's face. He stammered again. "What are you talking about, Stic?"

A left hand to Gappy's jaw sent waves of pain shooting through his skull and down his neck. Blood immediately found its way out the right side of Gappy's mouth. Gappy tried to shake off the dizziness but before he could recover, another stern blow to his face was delivered. Gappy saw stars for real. Darkness was trying to convey a message to Gappy's brain. But Gappy's eyes wouldn't close yet. His head was snatched upward and Stic got in his face.

"Gappy, I'ma ask you again. Who was you talking to about the Compound?"

"Nobody, Stic. Believe me. I ain't said nothing to no one about the Compound." Gappy mumbled through his swollen lip.

Stic turned to Skibop. "Tell this motherfucker what you heard!" Stic pointed at Gappy.

"Gappy, that bitch you got ain't shit. All I needed to do was buy that ass a drink or two at the club and promise her some of this here dick." He said grabbing his crotch, "I took that ass to the hotel and fucked her so good she started talking in tongues." Skibop mimicked.

Gappy narrowed his eyes at Skibop. "You dirty, motherfucker! You fucked my girl?! You fucked Ree Ree?" Gappy hissed.

"Man, Ree Ree is a straight up hoe. Shit, we all done hit that ass. Tell 'em Moop!" Skibop coaxed.

Moop concurred. "Yep, she's a straight hoe. She sucked the skin off my dick."

Stic interrupted, "Fuck what that hoe did to ya'll. Tell this motherfucker what that trick said."

Skibop replied, "Gappy, after I tapped that ass, Ree Ree described the Compound to me and told me that you brought her out here."

Gappy quickly scanned his memory and sure enough, he remembered telling her about the Compound. He was drunk and high and the promise of fucking her made him divulge information that he swore to secrecy. He quickly lied. "I didn't tell that bitch shit! She's lying man."

Stic chuckled. He stood in front of Gappy with his hands behind his back and leaned down over Gappy. "The only way that bitch could tell Skibop anything, is if she were told or saw it herself. And the only motherfucker who would have been stupid enough to tell her would be you, Gappy. You've always had a stupid side to you and now your stupidity has reared its ugly head again." With that said, Stic exploded with a series of quick left and right punches to Gabby's dome.

Barely conscience, Gabby tried to speak but he couldn't construct a coherent sentence. 'I…this…I don't…"

"Damon, bring me the Nitro, a hammer and tape."

Damon was standing in the background watching the reprimand of Gappy. Damon went to a secret door and unlocked it. He rummaged around until he found the Nitro, the hammer and the tape and brought them to Stic. Stic snatched the items eagerly from Damon's hands. Damon hated being called down to those types of meetings and he didn't like seeing that side of Stic. He watched with disdain as he stepped back into the background.

"This will do nicely." Stic remarked, as he held a large wide jar of liquid up in front of his face. Stic nodded his head at Moop.

Moop knew the nod. "I got it." He released the latch on the chair and pushed the back down. The chair stretched out like a table.

"Tape that lying motherfucker's trap shut." Stic commanded.

Moop took the duct tape and wrapped it around Gappy's mouth and chin and several times. His head was then taped down to the back of the chair to ensure immobility. Moop slapped Gappy a couple times to wake him up. Gappy's eyes opened wild with terror. Words nor sounds could escape his severely taped mouth. Stic unscrewed the top off the jar.

He leaned down in Gappy's face. "Oh yeah, I forgot to tell you, Ree Ree won't be talking to anyone about anything else. I cut that bitch's tongue out of her big mouth. Here, look for yourself." Stic withdrew a plastic bag from his shirt pocket and opened it. He poured the bloody contents of it on Gappy's face. Gappy's rapid eye movement said all that he could not say.

"You fucked up, Gappy and your services are no longer required. Because you drove that bitch out here, I'ma have to take your driving privileges away. Set his ass upright, Moop and take off his shoes."

Moop did as he was told. Beads of sweat ran down the sides of Gappy's face. He watched with confusion as Stic unscrewed the top off the jar and immediately visible vapors emerged from inside. Stic took Gappy's right foot and placed it in the jar of liquid. Gappy couldn't feel anything momentarily. Soon he felt a cold numbness begin to set within his foot and ascend up his leg.

What Stic wanted to happen wasn't happening fast enough so he repeated the process holding Gappy's foot in the liquid Nitrogen a little longer. This time, Gappy began shaking and thrashing in the chair. Skibop, Moop and Damon stared in disbelief as Gappy's left foot started to turn black and shrivel up. Stic was undaunted by the adverse reaction. Before anyone knew what was going to happen, Stic took the hammer and beat Gappy's foot. He didn't stop there. He took Gappy's right hand and placed it within the jar. It took on the same effects.

Stic took the hammer and beat Gappy's right hand with it. Gappy violently shook in the chair. He shook so hard he dislocated his shoulder. There were no words to describe the pain that tormented his body. He screamed through the tape for God to let him die. Damon turned his back away from the torture of Gappy. Moop and Skibop never saw Stic do anything so vile. Gappy was in shock. His body was shutting down.

Stic stood back and berated a slow dying Gappy. When he didn't die fast enough, Stic poured the remaining Nitrogen in Gappy's throat. Within minutes Gappy's esophagus was frostbitten beyond repair. His arteries froze quickly, shutting his supply of blood and oxygen. Gappy died a grueling death.

Damon shook the vivid scene from his head. He was in too deep and knew too much about Stic and his business. Leaving the Compound was out of the question. Stic would track him down and kill him. His sudden longing to be free was replaced with a sudden desire to live.

BIRTHDAY CAKE

"Happy Birthday, Cherry!" Betty and Aniya sang in unison to her. A huge chocolate cake with Butter cream icing proudly graced the center of the table.

"Make your wish, Diva and blow out them candles!" Aniya jeered.

With her cheeks full of air, Cherry blew out all the candles in one swoop. Betty and Aniya loudly clapped. After kisses and hugs were given, large slices of cake were served.

"So, I understand you two are going away for the week-end?" Betty said putting a large scoop of cake in her mouth.

"Yep, me and my favorite cousin are going to DC for the weekend. I can't wait." Cherry replied.

"That's right, I'm treating *my* favorite cousin to a weekend getaway, mom!" Aniya said hugging Cherry again. "And we're going to *Club Love* tonight, too." Aniya added, "So put down the rest of that cake girl cause I ain't trying to grease you up to put you in an outfit." She laughed.

"Nope, it's my birthday and I'm going to have this cake today!" Cherry returned. She took a huge piece of the cake and stuffed it into her mouth.

"So when do you guys leave, where are you staying and when are you coming back?" Betty asked giving both girls the eye.

"Mom?" Aniya whined.

"Mom, my ass! Give up the details. In case something happens, I need to know where my family is. So spit it out." Aniya wrote down the requested information for her mother. "Well you two have a wonderful time. Cherry baby, you certainly deserve this." Betty said. Before Betty left the kitchen she turned back to the giggling girls. "Tell Lukie and Tommie I said hello. Cause I know damn well their asses will be there, if they ain't there already!"

They both laughed having been called out. Some time later, outfits were thrown on the bed along with shoes and purses. Every available space was taken with several large suitcases in Aniya's and Cherry's room. After much deliberation, several carefully put together outfits were selected and ready to be packed. Aniya picked up a pair of jeans and screamed.

"What!" Cherry asked shaken at her cousin's sudden outburst.

"Look, there's a hole in the pocket. OMG! OMG! I can't wear these, Cherry! Shit, now I'ma have to run up to the mall and get another pair." Aniya exclaimed.

"Girl, you good and crazy! Ain't nothing wrong with those jeans. You can wear them just like that. You can't even see the damn hole and besides, that's the thing now. I've got a pair of holey jeans that I paid over a hundred dollars for. Stop tripping and put them things in the suitcase girl." Cherry cackled folding her underwear neatly in a pile.

"No, girl, I can't wear these. They weren't made with holes in them and I ain't gonna wear them with holes. Come on, Cherry, run with me to the mall!"

"No, boo. I got too much to do. Go ahead, we got plenty of time before we leave. I'ma finish packing. Do you want me to pack some of your big stuff?" Cherry asked.

"Yeah do that. I'm going to make a mad dash to the mall and come back." Aniya said. Five minutes later, Aniya was pulling into traffic in search of jeans.

Cherry continued to hum and pack for her birthday weekend, until she felt the phone on her belt vibrate. Her smile lit up the room when she saw Lukie's text. *I can't wait to be with you on this special night. Happy Birthday baby. I got something nice for you. I love you."* Cherry texted Lukie back.

"I can barely breathe because I am so excited. I can't wait either. I love you too!" She hit send and watched the little enve-

lope float to the middle of her screen as it pushed her message through to Lukie. After seeing the word “Sent” only then did she close her phone and put it back in the holder on her belt.

GARBAGE DISPOSAL

The door was snatched from her grasp after Bonita opened it. She was sickened when Stic and Moop entered. Stic walked in pushing Bonita back into the apartment. He and Moop looked around. "Look at this shit hole. It's hard to believe that a virgin actually lived here. Bonita, you're a fucked up housekeeper." Stic stated. He then spat on the floor.

"What do you want, Stic?"

"I come by to see how my Cherry pie is doing. I want me another slice." he sneered as he strolled around the tiny apartment.

He stopped when he stood in front of several pictures that were sitting on a dollar store étagère. They were of Cherry and Aniya. Bonita watched Stic pick up the pictures to study them for a few moments. Stic felt his dick rising in his pants. His mind filled with random thoughts of Cherry's tight pussy. He quickly put the picture face down.

"I don't understand what you're doing here."

"I asked you where was Cherry?" Stic said over his shoulder. Bonita didn't answer. Stic turned to face her. "Bitch, I'm talking to you! Don't make me go in my pocket on your ass." He threatened.

Moop stood at the door itching to slap a bitch. He was waiting for Stic's signal. Bonita offered no response to Stic. She was aware that this could mean her death but after what happened to Cherry, Bonita was now willing to lay down her life for her daughter. With a look of astonishment plastered on his face at

Bonita's defiance, Stic reached out and grabbed Bonita by her throat. He squeezed her throat and pulled her to his face.

"Bonita, I will kill you for sure. I need an answer to my question now, bitch!"

The air in Bonita's lungs was empting. Stic smiled as he watched Bonita fighting to breathe. Suddenly, he let her go. Bonita ran face first right into Moop's fist and crashed to the floor. She could feel her left eye beginning to swell. Moop immediately grabbed her by her arms and pulled her into the kitchen. Bonita kicked and twisted her body trying to extricate herself from Moop's death grip. Moment's later, Stic appeared in the kitchen.

"I just checked the bedrooms and it looks like my slice of pie packed up some shit and parted ways from you. Where did she go, Bonita!" he yelled.

Bonita did not answer. This only fueled his fire. He bent down and snatched her by the jaw. He was millimeters from her face. She could smell his funky breath of marijuana and scotch. She tried to move her nose away from him.

"I don't know where she is."

"Oh you on some ole 'save my daughter shit now', huh?" Stic laughed. "Do you really think that you are saving her by not telling me where she is? You really think I don't know where my Cherry pie is. I know she's been hanging over your sister's house. Come on, Bonita. I just wanted to see if you would tell me the truth before I go and get what's mine."

"Why don't you let her be, Stic? She's got her whole life ahead of her. I don't want her fucked up like I am." Bonita begged.

Stic didn't bother with a response to her plea.

"Look what I got in my hand!" Stic unfolded his hand and revealed the little black remote. "Forgot about this?"

"No Stic, please don't do it. My body can't take it." Bonita whispered.

"Huh? What did you say? You ain't begging a nigga is you?" Stic quipped "I don't know why the fuck I'm even wasting my time with your stupid ass. I was trying to be nice to a bitch but you want to play super mom and shit. It really don't matter because Cherry will be with me before the evening is over. I just wanted you to know."

"Stic, please, Cherry's all I got. Why don't you take me instead and let her live her life?"

"There you go trying to barter again. You ain't got nothing to barter with. Look at you, you're used up, you're a deadhead, you're poor, you're ugly, and I know that pussy is dried up. And I'll be damn if I let you put your snaggled tooth mouth on my dick. So what the fuck do you have to offer me? The way I see it," he paused, "shit, Cherry don't need you and probably never did. So she ain't losing out. If she loved you so much then where the fuck is she? I don't see her in here protecting you. Today is the day I'm collecting my invested property. Besides, your daughter got some sweet young pussy." Stic grabbed his dick, "And I can't wait to shove all this dick up in that tight ass too!"

Bonita hock spit in Stic's face. In a knee jerk reaction, he punched her in her face like a man. Bonita was out cold. Stic wiped the slimy goo from his nose and cheek as he ran over to the sink and rinsed his face.

"Bring that nasty motherfucker over here and stand her up." Stic commanded. Moop dragged an unconscious Bonita over to the sink. Both of them heaved her up from the floor and propped her against it. Stic nodded towards the switch for the garbage disposal on the wall.

"Check that!" Stic said.

He flipped it. "Looks like we're in business."

"Good, that's what I'm talking about. That's some proper shit! This bitch will never spit on another nigga again!"

Bonita's body was dead weight causing her to lean over on Stic for support. He looked at her with utter contempt and condescension. He immediately started slapping her all over her head repeatedly. He called her every foul thing he could think of while Moop burst out laughing. He thought watching Bonita's head bounce around on her shoulders like a ball, was the funniest thing. But Stic hated Bonita. He didn't know why but he hated this woman. Rage crept from somewhere deep inside of him and he needed to unleash it. He snatched one of Bonita's hands and put it in the sink and down into the hole.

"Go get something to tie her mouth up with." He commanded Moop.

"I found these." Moop returned to the sink with a pair of socks and a pair of panty hose.

Stic opened Bonita's mouth and inserted the socks. He took the pantyhose and stretched them twice around Bonita's mouth and securely tied it. Bonita was still out cold when Stic reached up and flipped the switch on the wall. The garbage disposal roared into action gnawing and grinding Bonita's hand. The sudden infliction of excruciating pain awoke her and was crippling.

Bonita could not fight off Moop and Stic as they continued to hold her and feed her hand into the disposal. All three of them looked like they were wrestling a snake in the sink. When the pain was too much, Bonita's body gave way to darkness. They released her, and she fell with a thud to the kitchen floor. Moop saw what was left of the bloodied, mangled atrocity that was once a hand and immediately grabbed his stomach and ran out the kitchen. He threw up his lunch of hot wings and fries onto the couch.

Stic walked around Bonita looking at her as if he was seeing her for the first time. His left foot automatically delivered a severe kick to her abdomen. Bonita didn't move. Stic moved around to Bonita's right side and delivered another strong kick to her ribs. Bonita didn't stir. Angered that she was not receptive to his punishment, Stic pulled out the remote and hit the button. He watched as Bonita's body convulsed on the floor. To him, she looked like she was doing the popcorn dance. He mocked her movements alongside her.

A sinister laugh escaped his throat as Bonita's body subsided. Spit and foam oozed from her mouth and ran down the side of her face.

"Stic, come on man we got other business to handle. And I need some air. Let's get the fuck outta of here." Moop said wiping his face with the back of his hand. He couldn't bring his self to look at Bonita anymore.

Stic pressed the button on the remote one more time. He could hear Bonita once again doing her dance on the floor. He never looked back as he and Moop left the apartment.

Frog paid for the pint of cheap gin and bounced out the store. He was going to head over to the bus stop and enjoy the pint of gin by himself but then he thought about Bonita. Maybe if he took her some, he might get lucky and she'd let him fuck. He twisted the cap on the bottle and made a U-turn to Bonita's house.

OPEN HOUSE

The Dodge Magnum rolled up on the right side of the garage. The door was left open after Aniya's hasty departure. She forgot to press the button to close it. Moop and Stic took advantage and were in the foyer of the house with their glocks drawn. They searched through it. Finding no movement on the first floor, they ascended to the next level. Betty was coming down the hall when Stic accosted her from behind.

He slammed his hand over Betty's mouth and pushed the barrel of his gun upside the back of her head. He whispered into her ear. "Move to the bedroom."

She moved along with Stic to her bedroom. Moop tossed a roll of duct tape to Stic and then stood guard at the door as Stic pushed Betty onto the bed and fell on top of her. He kept his hand over her mouth and his glock rested along side her temple. Betty was so scared she peed on herself.

Stic turned his head to Moop and whispered loudly. "Moop, get this bitch."

Betty began to buck under Stic's weight. When she saw his eyes narrow and felt the gun press harder against her temple, she stopped. Moop bound Betty with the tape and Stic gave Betty a double look. It was then that he remembered seeing her before.

"You's the same bitch that I was gonna pop at the red light when you damn near hit my car. Ain't this some shit. Is anybody else in here with you?" he asked.

Betty shook her head no. Stic chuckled. "I wouldn't lie if I were you. I already know she's here. I came to get what rightfully belongs to me. You can thank your skank ass sister for that."

Stic told Moop to keep an eye on Betty. He left the bedroom and went several feet down the hall. The first bedroom was empty. He crept up to the next open door and like magic appeared in front of an unsuspecting Cherry. When she looked up and saw Stic she screamed while looking for a getaway. With no way out except the door that Stic was in front of, Cherry raced to the window. She couldn't get it up fast enough before Stic hit her with the butt of his gun. Cherry fell backwards onto the dresser. She was about to move when Stic held up the device for Cherry to see.

She snarled lunged forward at Stic. He pressed a button and Cherry froze in mid air and began to twitch. Stic put the device in his pocket and half carried, half dragged Cherry down the hall, to her Aunt Betty's bedroom. Moop stepped aside as Stic pushed Cherry into the room. After binding Cherry's hands together and taping her mouth, Stic pointed at Betty.

"She looks just like your sorry ass mother don't she?" He looked at her. "Shit, them two bitches look like twins. Cherry, your mother ain't shit! She's the cause of this shit right here!"

Stic raised his glock and let off two rounds. One hitting Betty in the head and the other tore through her chest puncturing her heart. Death was swift for Betty and Cherry passed out.

ANIYA'S DISCOVERY

Aniya ran up the stairs to the house, with several bags in her possession. She was excited about her purchases. She bought two pair of jeans and two pair of shoes. She even bought Cherry a pair of sandals that she knew her cousin would absolutely adore. Aniya couldn't wait to show them to Cherry. She ran into the bedroom calling Cherry's name. Aniya noticed the suitcases and clothes were still unpacked. She didn't think much of it as she put the bags down on the bed. *Cherry's probably downstairs somewhere yapping on her phone with Lukie.* She thought.

Aniya pulled the jeans out the bag and pondered what shirt she could wear with them. She snapped her fingers and headed out the door. She was going to raid her mother's closet. Her mother was a trendy dresser just like her and Cherry, so finding a shirt to go with her jeans from her mother's closet was a synch. Aniya headed that way. And then she saw her mother.

A blood-curdling scream could be heard around the block as Aniya rushed to her mother and shook her. "Mom, please wake up! Mommy please…Nooooooo!" Aniya screamed. Her mother was dead.

Her mind was going a mile a minute and then she remembered Cherry. She ran out of the room frantically calling Cherry's name. She raced up and down the house looking in every room. Cherry had vanished into thin air. Aniya ran out on the porch where her screams summoned the next-door neighbor.

BUCKING THE SYSTEM

Cherry woke up in an unfamiliar setting. She groggily got out of the bed and looked around, as her eyes adjusted to the darkness of the room. She found the door and tried to open it. It wouldn't budge. She screamed at the top of her lungs for help. She beat her fists on the door until her hands hurt too much to move them. Defeated she slid down the door and onto the floor. Cherry refused to cry. She needed to keep her wits. She closed her eyes and thought about what had taken place and how she was going to get out of where ever she was alive.

While she looked for an escape, Dominitra went to check on Cherry and introduce himself. When he opened the door, Cherry ran through it. She had been waiting for this opportunity and there it was. Dominitra didn't give chase, instead he waited. Cherry didn't know the floor plan and found herself running in a circle right back to Dominitra.

"Stop running, Chile cause you're wasting your energy." Dominitra said calmly.

"Who are you and where am I?" Cherry asked.

"I'm Dominitra or Damon. It depends on what I'm wearing for the day." Dominitra explained. "And since I am dressed today in my newest Jovani couture dress you can call me Dominitra."

Cherry eyed Dominitra up and down. He was fully padded, face beat and the dress was one of a kind. "Am I at the drug dealer's house?" Cherry asked.

Dominitra exhaled noisily, "And which drug dealer are you referring to?"

"Don't play fucking games with me. You know who I'm talking about, the one that stole me and brought me here."

"Stole you?" He frowned.

"Yes, stole me. He broke into my aunt's house, killed her and took me. Now I'm standing here talking to a drag queen." Cherry sarcastically said.

"Well, I don't know about all that. I was told to make sure you, dear heart, were put into your room. I was also told to help you prepare to work." Dominitra replied.

"What do you mean, work?"

"You're about to become the next big porn star." Dominitra said waving his hands flirtatiously. "Whether you like it or not."

"Porn star? What the hell do you mean porn star? I'm not doing any porn movies for nobody." Cherry rebutted. "I don't know what's going on but I need to get out of here and back to my house. My cousin is probably going fucking crazy wondering what happened and where I am. She lost her mother, and now she lost me to." Cherry paused. "Oh my God, Lukie!"

"And who is Lukie?" Dominitra asked.

"He's my man, and when he finds out what the fuck happened, he's gonna come up in this bitch and light it up like the 4th of July!" Cherry hollered.

Not swayed by Cherry's statement, Dominitra moved towards Cherry and gently took her hand. Cherry snatched it out of Dominitra's grasp. "Get the fuck off of me! Don't touch me."

Dominitra cleared her throat. "Cherry, we need to talk."

"How do you know my name?"

"As I stated earlier, Stic told me about you prior to your arrival." Dominitra replied.

"Is that the bastard's name, Stic?" Cherry hissed.

Dominitra gave Cherry a nod and led her back into the bedroom. "Let me fill you in on some things." He informed.

After Dominitra's visit, where he explained everything she needed to know about the business, Cherry cried for several hours. She finally realized she was trapped.

Stic put the phone on the cradle and proceeded out the door. He called a meeting with the Compound that was urgent. When he reached the Pound, Stic took a quick head count to make sure everyone was in their seated positions when he walked in. Stic was the motherfucking King up in this bitch. Cherry was brought in unwillingly by Dominitra. Stic followed her around the room with his eyes, as Dominitra lead her to a seat that was front and center. With a dramatic wave of his hand, Stic began to speak.

"There's a new bitch in the family. Meet my Cherry pie, "he said licking his lips. Cherry rolled her eyes. Stic continued, "She's gonna be putting in work. I want you to welcome her to the family."

Cherry stood up. She opened her mouth to speak and Dominitra vigorously shook her head trying to forewarn Cherry. She defied his wishes. "I ain't puttin' in nothing! I didn't ask to come here and I damn sure don't want to be here!" Cherry narrowed her eyes and furloughed her brows. She pointed her finger at Stic and finished her defiance, "And I damn sure ain't doing no work here for you or no body else. And I don't care what you do to me, Stic!" Cherry spat staring intensely at him.

The look on Tawni, Trailer Trash and Carnival's faces were priceless. Tawni clucked her tongue. She waited for the wrath that she knew was going to be brought down on Cherry. She slowly eased her chair back to get out of the line of fire. Carnival wondered how Cherry would perform after the ass whooping that she knew Stic was about to deliver.

Big Blue was mad as hell because he knew he wouldn't be able to break Cherry in yet by making her get on her knees. He wanted a monster blowjob. He imagined her locs wrapped around his dick as he watched it go in and out of her mouth. He figured after Stic got done delivering her punishment, she was going to be laid up in the bed for a few days. And now he might have to ride across town somewhere to fetch a doctor for her.

Dominitra wanted to run up to Cherry and shake the shit out of her. He warned Cherry about Stic's sadistic and brutal ways. Cherry made the grave mistake of embarrassing him and talking back to him. Not only did she talk back, but she had the audacity to tell Stic she wasn't working. Oh, what a stupid ass thing to say.

Trailer Trash wasn't phased by any of what was taking place. The only thing on her mind was when was Stic going to give her another crypt of Mind Bend. Fuck all the rest of that shit. She wasn't interested.

"I think you're confused, Cherry." Stic sucked his teeth.

He looked at his manicured hands and blew out a long heavy sigh. He pushed his hands in his jean pockets and rocked back and forth on his Nike's. Then he slowly approached Cherry while she held her breath.

When she saw Stic put his hands in his pockets, she prepared herself for the seizure attack but instead, a hard slap to the right side of her cheek sent her spiraling over the chair. Before her brain could process the pain, she felt herself being pulled up by her locs and thrown on the couch. Stic wound his fist back and was ready to strike Cherry, when he felt his arm being stopped midway.

"Stic, come on, baby. If you beat her down now, she won't be any good to you later. Remember we need her for the shoot this week." Dominitra said.

Stic turned towards Dominitra and glared at him. He snatched his arm out of the grips of Dominitra's hold. "Everybody get the fuck outta here!"

No one needed to be told twice. They scrambled like roaches in a kitchen when the light was turned on. Cherry lay on the couch. She showed no emotion. Stic went to grab her when Dominitra stepped in again. "Let me take her, Stic. I'll make sure she steps in line." He didn't look convinced. "Please, Stic."

He looked at them both. "Dominitra, teach that bitch the rules. If you don't, the house will pay! Do I make my ass clear, nigga?"

"Crystal!" Dominitra replied.

Stic looked at his hands again, ensuring his manicure was still in tact. Nails filed and buffed to their natural luster. Stic took pride in the way his toenails and fingernails were presented to the world. He even had a personal manicurist on his payroll. He wasn't trying to call her talkative ass back to redo his shit. Cherry had better thank God his manicure was still right. He looked back at Cherry and Dominitra before he dipped out of the room.

Dominitra helped Cherry up from the couch. Cherry's face was swollen from the slap. Dominitra secretly thanked Jesus that he was there this time, to stop Cherry from being battered. He knew Stic would not have stopped beating Cherry until she was unconscious. Now he was going to be the one to whoop her ass for not listening to him, when she first came to the Pound. She told Cherry never to defy or argue with Stic. Stic always beat the girls within an inch of their lives.

"Your attitude is fucking with us all. I'm not going to always be there to save you. And if you keep this up, you'll need saving from me." He walked out for the moment, to leave her alone.

Cherry lie on her bed, with thoughts on escape, as her eyes darted around the room looking for exits.

Tawni, Carnival and Trailer Trash were gathered in Tawni's room. She spoke first. "Did ya'll see that shit? That bitch said some foul shit outta her mouth to Stic and all he did was slap her. Shit, I coulda slapped that bitch myself. How the fuck she just gonna get a slap?" Tawni was heated. "The last time I defied something that Stic told me to do, I woke up with two broken ribs."

"Yeah, I don't get that shit. Remember the shower incident and Stic broke my arm in several places because I didn't answer the phone right away." Carnival added putting her two cents in.

"But here's the motherfuckin' kicker, Dominitra's faggot ass gonna stop Stic from whooping her ass. What the hell was that about? That faggot motherfucker ain't never been to our rescue! And you know what, I ain't having it. I'ma find his punk ass right now and pull him up about that shit. I need's to know what that shit was about!" Tawni interjected rolling her neck.

"Shit, maybe he got a piece of Cherry's pie and he ain't gay no more!" Carnival giggled.

"Girl, that drag drama queen ain't go nowhere near no pussy. If we showed him ours, he would run outta of here screaming!" She laughed. "He don't know what to do with no pussy. Is you crazy?!" Tawni said seething.

The more she thought about Dominitra the madder she became. "Come on, Carnival, I'ma get to the bottom of this shit. Trailer, you coming with us?" Tawni asked.

"Never mind, you got the dumb ass look on your face and I ain't got none of that shit Stic be giving your crazy." She laughed. "So you stay right here. Matter fact, why don't you just face the wall and lick it! You can't even be help for the retarded. Damn! Come on, Carnival!"

Cherry stood at the caged window in her room and thought about Aniya. After seeing Stic kill her aunt Betty, she thought Aniya was probably in a mental ward somewhere. Aniya and her mother were close, unlike Cherry and her mother Bonita. She cried softly as her mind replayed Stic's shooting of her aunt in cold blood for no reason. No, wait, Stic said her aunt Betty looked like her mother. If she could kill her mother right now, Cherry wouldn't have given it a second thought. She gladly would do it.

As her mind raced, Cherry thought about Lukie. She wondered if he was out looking for her. Knowing Lukie, it wouldn't be long before he found her. Cherry's heart was breaking into a million pieces at the thought of not being with him. Her thoughts were halted when her door opened. She didn't like who she saw.

Stic stood in the shadow of the doorway. Her eyes met Stic's. He strolled in the room and stood in front of her. He threw a menacing stare. Cherry threw a stare back. "Umph." Stic said as he ran his fingers down the side of Cherry's swollen face. " I hated to do this to you." She slapped his hand away and Stic laughed. "I understand, baby girl. You don't want me touching you. But you can't forget that I've already touched you."

"No, I could never forget how you raped me you, sick motherfucker!" Cherry spat. "Call it what it is!"

"Well you can thank your fucked up mother for that!" Stic replied. Cherry remained silent. "And instead of dying like I asked a bitch to do, she traded your life to save hers. She gave you up like a bad habit. Oh my bad…wait…she didn't give that shit up either." Stic mused. "So now your mother's bill to me is what landed you here. So I'ma have to put a bitch to work. And, Cherry, you will be working on your back like the rest of these bitches in here. For the rest of your life."

"Why are you doing this to me? You should have just killed my mother. It would have put her out of her misery! And out of the drug infested life! Maybe then my aunt Betty would still be alive!" Cherry hissed.

Stic laughed at Cherry's statement about her mother. "You really would have wanted your mother dead?"

"I hate her." She looked out of the window again. "This is all her fault!"

"Damn, what kind of shit is that?" Stic chuckled. "That's cold, Shawty!"

"I could care less. She didn't care about me enough! She sold me to you for some drugs." Cherry replied. "My life is ruined for drugs!"

"Bonita couldn't sell a bottle of water. The only thing that bitch could sell was her pleads to me to save her life! And as far as your aunt went, she was expendable!"

"You fucking, monster! I'ma find a way to kill you!" Cherry seethed. "Before I die I promise I'll kill you!"

Stic got up in Cherry's face. His nostrils flared and the veins in his forehead bulged. He grabbed a handful of Cherry's locs and twisted her head to the side. With his other hand, he waved the device in front of her face. Stic grit his teeth and breathed in Cherry's face. "If I don't kill you first, bitch!" he growled. "You have to be slicker than snot to kill me, Cherry Pie.

You better be fucking careful about what you say. I don't take to being threatened lightly."

"Fuck you!" Cherry sternly whispered back in Stic's face. He forced her back against the window and slammed her head against the windowpane. Again he got in her face.

"I would love to fuck you again and I plan to do that. In the meantime, you're gonna do what the fuck I brought your ass here to do."

"I would rather die first. Just press the button, Stic." Cherry challenged. "Kill me! I'm dead already."

"Oh no, Princess, that would defeat the purpose of my plans. You're going to work, to pay for the sins of your mother."

"Fuck you and my mother!" He snapped her head and Cherry thought her neck snapped.

He slammed her head back up against the window and got in her ear. "Bitch, you belong to me now. And since I am your fuckin' daddy, you will do as I say. So let me make this perfectly clear, so that we ain't never got a problem again. Don't you ever talk back to me or defy my wishes. The very next time you step the fuck outta line, like you did today, you won't wake up for a week." He pushed her head against the window again. "I know that Dominitra told you the rules. Abide by them and your shit won't be lumped. I'ma leave your ass with one sure fact, your cousin and your boyfriend's lives now depend upon your performance." He sneered.

Cherry was scared now at the thought of Aniya or Lukie being harmed. Stic saw it in her eyes. "Please don't hurt them! Please!"

"That's what I thought!" he said as he slowly released her hair and backed away from her.

Cherry's tears streamed down her cheeks. She hated this man with everything she had. And the hate she felt in her heart for her mother, cloaked her like a thick heavy robe.

She breathed a short sigh of relief when he left. The only trace of Stic being in the room, was his cologne against her skin.

She ran to the bathroom to take the hottest shower she could, to remove his stench.

Tawni and Carnival accosted Dominitra while he was in the kitchen. He closed the refrigerator door and inhaled deeply. He put the bottle of soda on the counter and waited. Immediately, he felt a headache coming. What did these two fishtails want now? He knew it was some drama about him stopping Stic from hitting Cherry. Dominitra couldn't pen point what there was about Cherry, but there was something there that he liked, and he was going to protect her. Before Tawni and Carnival could get the words out of their mouths, Dominitra stepped to them. He waved his finger in the air and commenced to reading them.

"Before you two bring your funky tails in here, to discuss something that you both ain't got no business in or know anything about, I'ma stop you right here. This," he said, "is a wig." Dominitra pulled it off and threw it down on the floor. "Underneath here", he said pulling up his dress, "is my dick", he snatched it out of its hiding place and showed it to them. It sprang forward with force. "I'm still a fuckin' man. If you don't believe that I'm a man, why don't you both drop to your knees and suck it. Since I know its what you love to do." He paused. "I guarantee that I can cum on your faces just like those nasty ass men ya'll be fucking in them movies." Damon shook his dick at Tawni and Carnival. He added the last line of his statement. "And the ability to fight like a motherfuckin' man never leaves me. I suggest you two tramps make a U-turn and go back to where ever the fuck you came from."

When no one budged, Dominitra put his thick dick back in its hiding place under his dress. Both girls were dumbfounded. Neither one said a word at the sight of Dominitra's dick. The size and mass of it captured their attention completely and for the first time, neither Tawni nor Carnival had any words to say.

Dominitra snatched his wig off the floor and pushed himself between Tawni and Carnival damn near knocking Carnival's little ass to the ground as he left the kitchen.

WE NEED ANSWERS

Aniya couldn't get in her car fast enough. She put the key in the ignition and stomped on the gas.

"Damn, can I get in the car first?" Lukie said closing the door, as Aniya pulled off. "And slow the fuck down! Shit, you trying to kill a nigga." he hollered at Aniya.

She didn't pay Lukie any mind as she expertly maneuvered her car in and out of traffic. They were stopped at a red light on Liberty Road and when it turned green, the car in front of Aniya wasn't moving fast enough. Aniya laid on her car horn and began cursing at the car.

"Move, damn it! Come on! What fucking shade of green are you looking for?!" she yelled.

The driver in front threw his middle finger up in his rear-view mirror at Aniya. This only enraged her more. She pressed down on the accelerator and raced towards the vehicle. Lukie grabbed the dashboard for support as Aniya drove like a mad woman behind the wheel.

"Aniya!" he yelled, "I don't feel like beating nobody's ass right now or explaining to Tommie why we are in jail for road rage. So leave that mothafucka alone and let's go on to where we gotta go!" Lukie demanded.

"Did you see that smart mothafucka throw me the middle finger? Fuck that! I wanna whoop his ass!" She said still driving like a bat out of hell.

"Aniya, it ain't his ass you wanna whoop. So let's just go where we supposed to go and then you can put that whooping down on the correct ass." He replied. Aniya slowed the car down and headed towards their destination.

When they reached the place she couldn't wait to make it know she was there. Bang! Bang! Bang! Aniya hit the door with her fists like she was straight up 5-0. Aniya waited several minutes for the door to be answered and when it didn't open; she banged several more times. When she got no results, she added two kicks to the bottom for good measure. Locks could be heard being disengaged and a face peeped from behind the door.

"Open the door, aunt Bonita!" Aniya yelled.

"What do you want, Aniya, it's seven o'clock in the damn morning?!"

"I know what time it is. Let me in! I need to talk to you right now!"

"Aniya, I don't want to talk about shit right now. I'm tired and I'm going back to bed."

"Aunt Bonita, don't make me go get my boyfriend and his goons to come up in here and kick this bitch down. Now open this motherfucker right now, or so help me…"

"Shit!" Bonita exclaimed. As soon as she opened the door, Aniya rushed the door and stepped inside. Lukie followed behind. "And who is you?" Bonita asked.

Lukie didn't answer; he was too busy looking around the nasty apartment. He couldn't wrap his mind around the fact that his baby lived there. He sniffed the stale air that circulated throughout the apartment and wrinkled up his nose in condescension.

"Don't worry about who he is! I need to know what happened to Cherry! And don't tell me that you don't know anything about her disappearance because I know that's a goddamn lie!" Aniya spat.

"Who is you to be coming up in here questioning me? First of all you ain't grown enough to carry it like that with me, Aniya. I'm your aunt and…"

SLAP, SLAP!! Bonita was caught off guard with two quick slaps to her face. Bonita held the side of her face in disbelief that her niece just slapped the black off the left side of her cheek.

"Shut up, aunt Bonita before you get fucked up in this piece!" Aniya yelled. "I ought to beat your ass anyway just for GP. You are a piece of shit! Do you know that? You didn't even come to your own sister's funeral. And now your own daughter is missing and your ass hasn't been doing anything to find her. What kind of mother are you? I never dreamed in a million years that this shit could happen. My mother's dead and buried and my cousin is missing. I know in the depths of my soul that you're the culprit behind this!" Aniya spat.

Lukie moved from behind Aniya.

"Yo, if you know something about Cherry why can't you tell us, man? Are you being threatened?" Lukie inquired. "I got some boys that can handle that. Just tell us what we need to know! Please." Lukie begged.

"I don't know you, boy!" Bonita replied. "So don't say shit to me."

"I'm your daughter's boyfriend, Ms. Bonita. I love her and I just want to bring her home safely. If you know anything, please tell me. Please!" Lukie implored.

Bonita was caught off guard by Lukie's plea and the fact that he called her Ms. Bonita. She contemplated giving him a little info but then Aniya stepped in her face, pointing her finger and yelling. "If Cherry is out there alive somewhere and you let her die because you didn't come to her aid, I will personally come back here and kill you with my bare hands. Do you hear me, Bonita! I will fucking kill you myself!" She was so close in Bonita's face, spit sprayed from her mouth across Bonita's nose.

Lukie had to hold Aniya back by her other arm, as she continued to point her finger and woof at Bonita. "Maybe we should have let Cherry kill you that day! Maybe my mother would still be alive and my cousin would still be here." Aniya seethed.

Bonita had enough. She screamed at the top of her voice. "That's a mean and nasty thing to say to me, Aniya! Get the fuck out of my house! Both of you! Get the fuck out! I don't owe you shit, Aniya! Not a goddamn thing do I owe you or your dead mother! You and your mother always thought your asses were high and mighty." Bonita quipped.

Aniya snapped. She jumped on Bonita's back and began throwing wild punches to Bonita's head. Bonita tried to grab at Aniya but couldn't get to her. Bonita only had the use of one hand. The fighting pair fell into the doorway, causing Bonita's arm to hit the doorframe. Lukie pulled Aniya off her aunt's back and held her. Aniya cursed and screamed every obscenity known to man at her aunt. Bonita's bandaged arm was throbbing. Lukie pointed to Bonita.

"What happened to your arm? It's bleeding through the bandages." He said.

Bonita lifted her hand to inspect it. Blood was beginning to soak within the folds of the bandage. "Aunt Bonita, what happened to your hand?" Aniya asked.

Bonita thought quickly. "I cut my hand and gangrene set in. It has to be cut off." Bonita whispered.

Bonita stared at her aunt's blood soaked bandaged arm. She didn't feel any remorse for her. "Whatever! You deserve it!" she said. Aniya kicked open the door and her and Lukie bounced.

Bonita had been a bag of nerves ever since hearing of Betty's death and Cherry's disappearance. Stic did another one of his magic acts and appeared in her home the day before Betty's funeral. He told Bonita there were too many people around that would question her about Betty and Cherry. It would be in her best interest if she stayed home.

Now Aniya showed up with Cherry's boyfriend demanding answers that Bonita knew she couldn't give. Bonita's world had crumbled. In the process of trying to save herself, she cost her sister her life and now Cherry was God knows where with Stic, doing God knows what. She might not ever see Cherry again.

Maybe Frog should have let her bleed to death that day he came in and found her on the floor unconscious. How in God's name did she let this happen? She knew she would have to answer to God for this grave mistake. And probably sooner than later.

LOW KEY

Several weeks went by and Cherry could not find an escape route or devise a plan that was full proof. During that time, Stic forced Cherry to act in his movies. With Cherry being the newest porn queen in his stable, Stic's movie sales picked up and Cherry became a hot commodity.

Over the course of time, Cherry and Damon became close. Damon learned about Cherry's life and she learned a little about his. When Cherry told Damon about Stic raping her in front of her mother, Damon was livid. There was something so wrong with a man taking a woman by force like that. Damon hated men who did that. But Damon was confused when Cherry told him about the device that Stic used on her and her mother.

Damon decided to question her more. "Chile, I'ma need for you to tell me some more about this so called gadget that Stic has, cuz he damn sure ain't used nothing like that on anyone else here."

"I'm telling you the truth, Damon. Stic somehow, someway put something in my body that makes me have convulsions. When he presses the button on the trigger box, it fucks my body up. My mother had the same thing done to her."

"Did he drug you or something? Didn't you know that you were having this thing implanted in you?"

"No, Damon, all I remember was being at home reading when someone burst into my house and put something over my nose and mouth. Whatever it was knocked me the fuck out. The next thing I knew, I woke up in some room that looked like it was made of plastic."

He knew exactly what room Cherry was talking about. He let her continue.

"My mother was bound to a chair. Stic pulled out some little black device that looked like a ring that car keys are made for and he pushed a button. My body went into a seizure and…" She trailed off momentarily and then through clenched teeth she said, "then that mothafucka raped me in front of my own mother."

Cherry stopped talking again and stared off into space. Images of Stic raping Cherry ran rampant in Damon's head. It was bad enough that Damon learned about Trailer Trash, now she just found out about Cherry. The difference was Trailer Trash liked being rape. She was just as sick as Stic.

Damon was mad. Mad because he loved Stic and Stic was raping women left and right. Why couldn't that mothafucka just be happy with him? Why? Damon was feeling some kinda way.

Cherry spoke again, breaking Damon's thoughts. "Are you sure that no one else has this thing in them? I mean can you really be sure?"

"I can't be sure, Cherry. But I've never seen any of them have a fit either. Only Trailer Trash snaps the fuck out when she's high and when she ain't high. But she don't be having no seizure or nothing like that." Damon confirmed.

"What about you? Are you sure you don't have the problem?"

Damon cocked his head to the side and put his hand up for emphasis. "Don't you think that I would know if my ass had some type of device or bug planted on me? I ain't never had any operations or nothing like that."

"Well consider yourself one lucky bitch then." Cherry replied.

Damon made Cherry strip off all her clothing and he examined every inch of her body. There was nothing to be found. No marks, no scars, no incisions...nothing. Damon wondered if Cherry was exaggerating.

"I don't see anything, baby. Are you sure?"

"You gotta believe me. I'm telling you the truth."

He left her room and went back to his. He thought about what Cherry said about being knocked out and not remembering anything. He went through his mental Rolodex and recalled one time that he got sick.

He was feeling good one minute and the next minute he was sick as a dog. Damon replayed the way Stic took care of him. And then a bolt of horror ran through Damon's chest. When Damon got sick it was on a Tuesday. It was Thursday evening when Damon woke up from his fever and didn't remember shit. Stic told him that he had been sleep for two days with a fever. At the time, Damon believed Stic but now after listening to Cherry, he wondered if Stic drugged him and did something to him too. But if Stic did, wouldn't he have done something by now? Wouldn't he know if he was implanted with the same thing?

Since Damon never had any episodes like the ones Cherry described, he dismissed the thought. At the moment, his worry was on the fact that Stic hadn't called him, nor had there been any more discussions about them going away together. What was up with that? He was going to find out what his man was up to.

He needed to talk to Stic immediately. Ready or not.

THREE THE HARD WAY

Lukie, Aniya and Tommie were practicality inseparable over the past weeks. Lukie and Aniya were each other's strong hold and they developed a tight bond. Aniya knew Cherry's disappearance had something to do with her mother's death. Every resource they could find, they used to get answers to Betty's death and Cherry's disappearance. Aniya even told the police about the Magnum car. And how Cherry was scared, when it showed up down the street from her house. But Aniya couldn't give an accurate description of Stic because she didn't pay him any attention. All she knew was that when he appeared, Cherry had the seizure.

The police hadn't turned up with anything. And the car could not be found because there was no record of a license plate or a bill of sale. Aniya blamed herself repeatedly for her mother's death. If she had closed the garage door, the intruders would not have been able to get in so easily. Of course, Bonita was questioned and she gave up no information. Stic knew he had to cover his tracks, which is why he made sure that if Bonita spoke, she'd loose her tongue soon after.

Stic stood in the filthy living room of Bonita's apartment. The only soldier he had with today was his Glock and it was aimed at Bonita. "I know the police been round here askin' questions and shit. From what I understand you kept your mouth shut." He paused and waited for Bonita to speak. “I guess you follow rules good after all.”

She shrugged her shoulders. Bonita had no more words left for Stic and at this point she didn’t care whether she lived or died. That was, until an image of Cherry raced through her mind. “How is my daughter?” She softly asked as she looked up at Stic. “Is she okay? Is she hurt? Please don’t hurt her, Stic.”

Stic took the toothpick out of his mouth and pointed it Bonita. “Oh that sweet thang is good. She’s making me money. Lots of it.”

“What is that supposed to mean?”

“It means Cherry’s doing just what I told your stupid ass she was going to do. Earn. She’s one of the hottest pieces of ass on my payroll! I line ‘em up and Cherry lies ‘em down.”

“But she’s a virgin.”

“She ain’t a virgin to shit no more! Remember?” He laughed. “She can fuck ‘em standing on her head now!” Stic mocked. “Your little girl left when I stuck her with this cock.”

Bonita put her hands to her ears and covered them. “Please, Stic, I can’t bare this.” Bonita whispered. “I just can’t. I don’t want to hear anymore.”

“What…you can’t handle the truth! You should be proud of Cherry. She’s in some of the finest porn movies I make!” Stic continued. “Congratulations, Bonita, you have a star in the family.”

Bonita dropped to the floor in a heap. She rocked her body back and forth all the while muttering to herself. Stic put the toothpick back in his mouth. He looked down at a snibbling Bonita. With the barrel of his Glock, he pushed her in the back of the head. “Man the fuck up! This shit is your doing. Both you bitches ain’t bodied so what the fuck you crying for?”

“Stop telling me what I already know! I don’t want to hear anymore!”

He could have easily killed Bonita long ago, but she might serve a purpose later so he decided to let her live. Stic put his Glock in the holster under his arm and pulled his jacket closed.

"Please let her go, Stic. Let me be in your porn movies."

He turned his lips up in utter disgust. He went to the door and grabbed the knob. He twisted it just enough to get it open. He kicked the door wider with his foot and walked out. "Nasty, bitch!" he said out loud. "Your washed up ass couldn't be in anything I produce."

"I don't know what happened to you, but if you don't get it together, it may be your undoing."

"Spoken from a washed up addict." He laughed. "Remind me to take your advice, after I wipe my ass with it."

PORN STAR

"Tommie, do we have to see another one of those sleazy ass porn movies? Damn, boy, you must spend oodles of money on those things." Aniya teased as she undressed for bed.

"Naw, boo. Ole Boy on the job get's 'em for me. He sells them five for twenty bucks. Shit, you can't beat that. Before Ole Boy came with his hustle, I was buying them joints straight from the store. Them bitches was almost forty dollars a pop. Shit, Ole boy be giving me the hook up. You can't tell these from the real deals."

Aniya put on one of her favorite Teddy's and climbed into the bed. She positioned herself under Tommie's arm. They cuddled and kissed while trying to watch one of the latest DVD's that Tommie acquired from his connect. Soon, Tommie and Aniya were engaged in lovemaking while the movie became the background noise. Aniya was trying to concentrate will riding Tommie's dick but the noise in the movie was getting on her nerves.

"Tommie, turn that shit off. It's interrupting my ride." She giggled. "Why watch that shit when you have the real thing?"

Tommie felt around the bed for the remote but it was not there. Aniya continued to ride his dick. Tommie grabbed her by the waist and thrust deep into her wetness. Sounds of making love rebounded off the walls. Aniya was just about ready to pop her shit off, when one of the voices on the movie screamed, breaking Aniya's concentration. She pulled herself off of Tommie's dick and looked for the remote.

"Damn, baby, what you doing? Shit you messing me up." Tommie complained. "That shit was feeling too good."

"This fucking whack ass porn movie is messing me up, Tommie. Where the hell is the remote? Because you 'bout to make me dry up."

"I don't know, baby. Look over on the dresser. I think I put it there." He answered.

Aniya's phat to death jiggley ass, bounced up and down as she leaped off the bed and headed towards the dresser. Tommie licked his lips in admiration. He couldn't wait to finish planting his seed in that thang.

Aniya found the remote and turned towards the TV to press the button. She glanced at the picture on the screen and then walked over to the TV. Something about the person looked familiar. When she leaned in, she knew exactly who it was. She stood in front of it with her mouth gapped open. Her jaw almost hit the floor. "Tommie…Tommie…Come here! Look…Look!" Aniya shrieked. "Look!" she pointed to the TV. "That's my cousin! That's my people!"

Tommie slid down to the bottom of the bed and his eyes fell on what Aniya was pointing to. Both Tommie and Aniya looked at one another incredulously.

"I gotta call Lukie! I need to let him know!"

GEARIN' UP

Lukie couldn't stand to watch any more of the movie. Seeing Cherry performing sexual acts with other men made his stomach wrench. Aniya knew it was hard for Lukie to watch so she stopped the DVD and ejected it. It wasn't like he didn't get the point. When they were done, all three sat on the couch in silence.

"I can't believe this. What's going on? Lukie's face was in his hands.

"I know, Lukie, and I'm so sorry." Aniya cut her eyes at Tommie who was shaking his head in pity.

"Tommie, man, where did you get that DVD?" Lukie quizzed. "I need to get in contact with whoever made that shit."

"From one of my connects at work who makes pirated movies." Tommie replied.

"Did it have a cover on it?"

"Yeah, but it wasn't the original cover. It was one of the color printed kind. Let me get it."

Tommie came back with a piece of paper used as a cover and handed it to Lukie. He looked at it front and back. The paper didn't reveal much of anything. "This is not telling me shit! I need more!"

"Go back to the beginning of the movie and look at the credits. I'll write everything down." Aniya offered.

Tommie pushed the DVD back into the player and started it from the beginning. Like children in a classroom, each of them watched the movie and read the credits in the beginning and at the end. All three physically and mentally took notes. Lukie's feet kept rocking and wouldn't keep still. He wanted to snatch Cherry out of the movie and whoop her ass for hurting him. How could she do this? She was supposed to be his girl. They were supposed to go away for her birthday weekend. But instead, she up and disappears for weeks without any contact what so ever. Now she shows up on Tommie's fucking DVD for Christ's sakes. He was humiliated and embarrassed he ever tried to wife her.

"Lukie, if you ask me, something is up." Tommie said. "This doesn't feel right."

"I'm with him. This is wrong. I know my cousin, she isn't like this." She looked at him. "Are you okay?"

He didn't know how to feel. His emotions took him from being sad to hurt, to wanting to choke the very life from Cherry's body. At this moment in time, Lukie was livid. "Yo, you get all that shit down, Aniya?" he barked.

Aniya whipped her head up at Lukie. "Yo, what's wrong with you?" Aniya snapped back. "I'm on your side! Remember?"

Lukie walked away from the TV and began to pace in front of Aniya. "I'm sorry but I can't fucking believe what I just saw, Aniya!"

"Like I said, something is off."

"You can't be sitting there not feeling like whooping Cherry's ass too." he challenged.

"Lukie, Cherry ain't making these movies on her own. Someone is making her do them. Look at her. You could tell she was putting on an act. She don't even look like herself. She looks forced. That's not Cherry." She pointed at the TV. "I know my cousin, Lukie. Something has happened to make her do that shit."

Lukie turned and faced Aniya. "Maybe you don't know that bitch like you thought you did." He shot back.

"Whoa, hold up. First of all Cherry is still my peoples," Aniya pointed to her chest for emphasis, "and I ain't gonna let you or nobody else call her out her name. I damn sure ain't gonna let you talk shit 'bout her."

"But how can you be sure?"

"I don't know. I just know my fucking cousin. Never once has she ever mentioned or even thought about being in no porn movies. And you should know this yourself. She was a virgin, Lukie! Didn't you know that?"

Lukie immediately thought about the first couple of times he tried to touch Cherry and she would zone out on him. Maybe that was the reason. She never had sex and now Aniya was telling him that he was her first. "Aniya, are you sure that Cherry ain't been with no other man?" he questioned.

"Yo," Tommie interjected, "remember the day we all went out for burgers at the 50's joint at the mall?"

"Yeah," Lukie replied.

"Well Aniya told me then that Cherry was a virgin. But then you and Cherry let the cat out the bag that ya'll had smashed each other and it was official that Cherry was no longer green. You were the first man to plant a flag on her planet, dude."

"I can't believe it." He rubbed his head. "I can't fuckin' believe it. I was her first? Damn. Look here ya'll, we need to find out all we can about this production company and fast. Cherry's life might be dependent on us!" Lukie didn't need any more convincing.

"Yeah, you right. Let me put some feelers out in the street and see what we catch on the lines. In the meantime, Lukie, let's get our gear tight. We might have to lay a few nigga's down." Tommie instructed.

"You know I'm with it!"

DISAPPOINTED DAMON

Damon was in the main house with Stic. Stic was giving him a laundry list of shit he wanted done around the Compound for the next movie. Damon typed everything down in his iPad. When Stic finished throwing commands and demands, Damon powered down the iPad.

He took a deep breath, in preparation to address Stic. "So, when do we leave for our mini vacation, babe?"

Stic didn't respond, he was busy looking at his text messages. The last thing he wanted to hear was Damon's bellyaching about going away with him.

"You heard me, baby?" Damon got up and sat beside Stic on the couch. He put his arm around Stic's shoulder. Stic instantly recoiled from Damon and stood up to finish reading his texts.

Damon was rattled as he sat on the couch, embarrassed by Stic's display of ill will towards him. But he decided to try again from a different angle. "Stic, honey you've been working your ass off. You've acquired a new porn star and the production company practically runs itself. Why don't you let me book us a fancy all inclusive hotel for next weekend?" Damon said.

"I'm not going anywhere, Damon. I've got several business deals lined up and I need to make sure these buyers is bringing the right numbers to the table." Stic replied without so much as looking at Damon.

He frowned. "Can't Moop or Skibop handle that?"

Damon knew he fucked up when that statement slipped between his teeth and landed in Stic's ears. Stic stopped texting and put his phone down at his side. He stared intensely at Damon.

"Nigga, I know you just didn't suggest that I let Moop or Skibop handle my money, let alone my business deals. Is you crazy, mothafucka? Why don't you just continue doing what you do best. Just be my bitch when I need you to be and play mommy to those whores at the Pound."

"But you said we would get away."

"Read my lips and hear what I'm saying, I am not going anywhere with you Damon, not now or ever. I have no desire to be with you like that. Now, do you have any other comments to add or any more suggestions to make?" Stic asked.

"No, Stic. I have all the answers I need." His head throbbed.

He sniffed hard and blinked back tears that threatened to roll down his perfectly beat face. Damon wasn't in full drag but his face was always made up. He was not about to let Stic see him cry.

"You need to be happy for what I do for you around here." Stic went back to texting and turned his back to Damon. He heard the door close upon Damon's departure. "Fucking pain in the ass faggot!" He said out loud.

STOLEN JOHN

Damon came back to the Pound to find Trailer Trash and Carnival arguing. He put his head down and shook it because now was not the time to have to deal with the two fish tails. He was still trying to digest what Stic just told him. The more he thought about it, the angrier he became.

He was snapped out of his thoughts as glass could be heard shattering in the background. Damon hit the corner of the kitchen just in time to snatch a glass out of Carnival's hand. With a quick glance, Damon scanned the mess. Glass was everywhere.

"What the hell?" Damon shouted.

Before he could get his next word in, Carnival and Trailer Trash began shouting at one another again.

"You funky, bitch!" Trailer Trash yelled.

"You horse fucking, whore!" Carnival retaliated.

Damon couldn't make out the rest of what was being said, so he stepped in between the two. Damon pushed Carnival's midget ass away from Trailer Trash who was nicked with cuts. Apparently from the shrouds of glass that burst on the wall behind her. From the looks of it, it appears that Carnival was the aggressor in this match.

"Damon, you better get that crazy white girl or I'ma set fire to her ass!" Carnival shouted.

"Fuck you, Carnival!" Trailer spat back. "I didn't steal your fuckin' John. I'm tired of you fucking with me."

"Yes you did you lying, bitch!" Carnival yelled. "You will fuck anything and anybody! I hate you so much!"

"Shut it up! What the hell is going on in here?!" Damon hollered. "I hear a bunch of yapping but no talking. Now either tell me what the fuck is up, or I'm gonna start snatching some heads in here."

"Carnival thinks I stole her John." Trailer Trash started. "But I didn't steal shit. He requested another girl so Carnival came and got me. I was minding my business!"

"I don't understand."

"She thought he wanted two girls. But the John didn't want to fuck Carnival. He told Carnival to watch. And now she's mad! It's not my fault!"

"Who got paid?" Damon asked. "That's what the fuck I want to know."

"I did. I'm that one that fucked him!" Trailer Trash replied. "And that's why he paid me. I did the duty not that booty."

"No bitch, you were supposed to split the money with me. You wouldn't be paid shit with your chronically high ass, if I didn't come fetch a bitch." Carnival pointed out. "And now you trying to keep all of the cash for yourself."

Damon had enough of the catfight. He was tired of putting out stupid ass fires like these. He snatched Trailer Trash by the arm and peered into her face.

"I don't care who fucked who, who sucked who, or whose pussy did the work. I'm sick of this shit with you bitches in this house. I don't feel like it today. Because guess what, this evening, I have something on my mind! Now, how much did you get paid, Trailer?" Damon snarled.

"Two…two hundred dollars…and," Trailer Trash stammered before Damon cut her off.

"You are going to give Carnival a hundred dollars of that money, now!" He said digging his manicured fingernails into Trailer Trash's forearm.

Damon's eyes were glazed over with hostility. He was not to be fucked with at the moment. Dominitra was nowhere to be found. This was straight Damon the man. And if plucked, he was gonna show each of these bitches just who Damon really was. Even Carnival shut her mouth and backed her little ass up towards the door. So in case a nigga got stupid, she had running room.

"Did you hear what I said, Trailer?" Damon asked jarring her arm. "Or do I have to make you feel me?"

"Yeah, I heard you, Damon. Now let me go. You're hurting my arm." she whined.

Damon slowly released his grip of Trailer Trash's arm. "Clean up this shit in here. And put some money on the counter for these broken glasses, Carnival."

Damon marched out of the kitchen back to his room. He was sick of this shit and sick of being treated like a doormat by Stic. Something had to give.

VIP

Stic just finished placing an order with his production company for another two thousand-five hundred copies of one of Cherry's movies. He hadn't fucked Cherry since she'd been there. He was saving her for a special scene of his own but mostly because he was too busy in the streets producing Mind Bend.

The drug spread across the country like a plaque and Stic was at an all time high. Money flowed in like water flowing from a faucet and his porno movies were once again in rapid demand. Instead of Trailer Trash, Cherry was leading the way.

Tonight some special ballers were coming into town. He was going to take Cherry with him to the private location. He wanted to show off the power he had over her, with her implanted device. This was the next branch in his tree of entrepreneurship.

He rang The Compound. Tawni picked up the phone on the first ring.

"Tawni, I need Cherry to get ready for VIP's tonight, you heard me?" Tawni snarled her face up. She didn't want Stic to hear her anger so she put on her best voice.

"Sure, Stic. Are there any other requests?"

"Naw, no other requests tonight." Stic replied. Tawni gave a staggered pause, Stic caught it. "Tawni, stop fucking wasting my time, what's on your mind? I can hear your head rattling through the phone.

Tawni bucked up. "I hate to bother you."

"Stop wasting my time! Get to it!"

"Well, it's just that no one has been requesting me lately, especially now that Cherry done came up in here. It seem like she's taking my business and I ain't feelin' that, Stic. And you…"

Stic wasn't trying to hear her whining. He cut her to the quick. "What the fuck I tell you and all them hoes to do? Huh? What the fuck I tell you?"

"I...you said..."

"Didn't I tell you that you need to come up with some new shit? Ya'll need a marketing plan."

"But I don't know how."

"It's easy. Learn how to market yourselves so that the demand is greater than the supply. You do that and motherfuckers will be beating down the door to own a copy of your shit."

"I'm trying..."

"Trying ain't good enough! How the fuck you think you gonna sell something when you ain't got no gimmick? Tawni, you got a big ass but you can't move it like you used too. Learn how to roll them ass cheeks on a nigga's dick and you ain't got to worry about requests. Shit, them motherfuckers will beat their meat sitting in front of the TV watching you work that ass. Shit, all ya'll need a fuckin' makeover and some new gimmicks."

"Okay, Stic. I understand."

"Work that shit out with Dominitra. Now I got shit to do."

Tawni didn't hear anything else but a dial tone.

Tawni headed towards Cherry's room. She hated Cherry. There was nothing about her that Tawni liked. As much as she didn't want to tell Cherry that Stic was taking her to VIP's tonight, she knew better. Stic didn't give a shit about whom you liked in the Pound or who you didn't like. If he sent a message, that shit had better be delivered. He held the whole house accountable for each other's actions. When one fucked up, they all fucked up.

She knocked on the door and Cherry opened it. She didn't greet Tawni with any salutations. This was another reason Tawni hated Cherry. First of all, Stic put her in the big ass room on the other side of the hallway, like she was a damn queen and shit. And then she opened the door and didn't even say hi to Tawni. They both stood there looking at each other. Cherry ghetto stanced and cocked her head to the side. She folded her arms and waited.

Tawni looked Cherry up and down before she delivered Stic's message. "Stic said you're going to VIP, be ready, bitch!"

"Don't be mad at me, Tawni cause for real, I don't want to go to no fucking VIP."

"Whatever, Cherry."

"For real! I hate this shit, and everyone here too." She put her hands on her hips. " And that includes your ass."

"Don't push me. I'm not your friend."

"Whatever. If you want the job, by all means call that crazy motherfuckin' Stic and tell him you're going in my place. When they get done putting you in a full body cast, I bet your big ass won't be mad no more!" Cherry slammed the door in Tawni's face.

SHOWTIME

Big Blue led a handcuffed and guillotine hooded Cherry into a room. He seated her on the bed and removed the handcuffs followed by the hood from over her head.

"Stic is greeting the VIP's, you know where I'll be." He said.

"I don't give a fuck." Cherry said.

She inspected the room. It was Moroccan infused with hints of Africa thrown in. Strong incense permeated through out the room. The only lights in the room were from several large candles placed in hurricane holders that were randomly placed about the space. How befitting that Cherry chose to wear something exotic.

She wore an outfit that resembled a belly dancer's outfit. The top was midriff and jeweled fingers hung from around it. Her hip hugger pants sat low on her waist and the wide legs of the jeans made them look like a long skirt. Her waist was adorned with a jeweled belly chain.

As much as she hated Stic and starring in his porno movies, she did take the money. She was stashing all of it to use when she escaped from the Compound. She still didn't have a plan, but she was going to find a way to get the fuck out of Stic's Compound for good. Cherry didn't have a choice about doing the movies. Stic pushed her button to make her do what he wanted her to do.

When Cherry first objected to Stic's demands, he served her with pain so bad that she couldn't get out of bed for two days. As she began to succumb to Stic's requests, he lessoned the beatings. When she would shoot her movies, Stic was on the set each and every time ensuring that Cherry gave a stellar performance.

Stic's tracking and control implant was one of the best investments he ever made. Today Stic was going to make new power deals with the same technology.

Cherry assumed she was waiting for one of Stic's rich friends to come in and request some far side shit, as a lot of the VIPs were eccentric. Every man was different and so were their requests. Most of her requests were for S&M with her being the master. She hated doing it because it involved hardcore toys that either she or they had to wear. Her worst were the collars with attached nipple clamps. They bruised her neck and made her nipples sore for days.

Then there was the arm binder or arm splints that locked behind her back, causing her arms to be immobile during sex. Other toys of torture were the mouth harnesses that were either muzzle or gag style. Of course there was always the whips and paddles, leg and arm bondages. And how could she ever forget the time she went to a VIP outing at a millionaire's house and he had a slave driver fucking machine and a fuck saw? After her encounter with the machine and the saw, she could not work. Her pussy was so raw and swollen, Dominitra had to call a doctor to come to the Pound.

When Stic found out that his best moneymaker couldn't make his porno movies, he hit the roof. He sent Skibop and Moop over to the millionaire's house for blood. After beating him damn near to death, Moop took a broom handle and shoved it up his ass over and over until the muscles in his rectum were torn to shreds.

Finally Stic rolled in the secret location with several VIP's trailing behind him. Stic didn't deal with anyone under the ten million dollar earning mark. If you didn't make ten million or more, Stic didn't fuck with you like that. Cherry was the only one of the girls at the Pound that Stic took out on the town to secret locations and forced her to be with these types of people.

Gurkha's "His Majesty's Reserve," cigar smoke swirled around the heads of Stic and three other money movers in the room. Each man toasted with a glass of Louis XIII Cognac. Everyone was waiting to see what Stic had planned for their entertainment tonight. After pulling back the curtains on the two-way mirror, Stic and the others saw Cherry sitting on the bed.

"Gentlemen, meet Cherry. She is about to perform for you like you've never seen a bitch do." He spoke into a microphone on the side of his chair.

"She's quite lovely." One of them said.

"Only the best." He looked at her. "Cherry, stand up." Cherry did as requested. "Dance for me." Stic commanded.

Cherry started to dance. She swayed her hips from side to side and moved her hands and arms in an erotic movement. The men ogled at Cherry. Once Stic had their attention, it was time to bring in the big guns.

"Damn that bitch bad." One of them said.

"Dance faster." Stic said into the mic.

Cherry did as instructed and started to move faster. There was no music playing in the room so Cherry had to dance to a song in her head. Stic produced his device and waved it around so everyone could see it.

"Gentlemen, watch this."

With that, Stic pressed a button and Cherry stopped dancing and began to jerk and twitch where she stood. Gaston the Greek almost choked on his Cognac. He leaned forward in his chair in astonishment at Cherry's behavior.

"You make her do this, no?" He said to Stic in his thick Greek accent.

"Yes. I have complete control over her. Watch some more."

Stic tapped the button again and Cherry's movements became more rigid and severe. Stic didn't want to go too far with the demonstration because Cherry had to be ready for her movie shoot in the morning. Stic released the pressure off the button and Cherry's movement stopped. She dropped to her knees along side the bed, trying to gather her wits about herself. She didn't expect Stic to use the device on her while she was out. Her body and mind was weakened by Stic's display of power to his comrades.

"What is this, man?" One of them looked at the box in his hand with astonishment.

"And how do we get one of those?" Asked another.

More eager discussion was made about the device. Questions included how to get it, who would install it and who they could use the device on. Stic answered each question like a game show contestant.

Gaston the Greek was already calculating the cost. It was well worth his money to get the information from Stic. Gaston wanted to make sure that this was no fluke so he asked to use the device himself. Stic handed the device over to Gaston with instructions.

Gaston felt the design in his hand. It resembled a key faub. Gaston aimed the device at Cherry through the window and hit the button. Immediately Cherry started to jolt and spasm beside the bed. She was still on her knees when the second round of tremors tore through her body. Pleased with the display of authenticity, contracts for the apparatus were drawn. The round table of happy owners left the premises with nothing on their minds except controllability of another person.

When the meeting was over, Stic summoned Big Blue. Cherry was cloaked in concealment from the outside world and taken back to the Compound. She was starting to wonder if she'd ever get away from this lifestyle.

PRIVATE SHOWINGS

Tommie and Lukie were in the mall headed towards the food court. They were walking past a *Victoria's Secret* store when Tommie stopped dead in his tracks. He backed up and searched the store. His eyes nervously darted to every woman he saw. Then his eyes blossomed.

"Oh snap, Lukie. I know her!"

"Nigga, who you talkin' about?" Lukie asked now looking in the store with Tommie.

Tommie pointed to a lady who was bent over looking at panties. "I know that chick. Wait, let me think…um, that's right, man, she's in one of them movies I got at home!"

"What?" he raised is brows. "Tommie, you sure about that man?" Lukie asked hoping like hell Tommie was on point.

"Man, I can't forget her face and her ass. She got the world's biggest." He observed her body. "Wait 'till she turns around."

Tawni turned her back towards Lukie and Tommie to get a better look at a robe that was hanging on the display. Like a church choir, both of them sang out, "Dammmn!" When Tawni's ass pointed directly at them.

"Man, we need to check that bitch out right now!" Lukie said.

Tommie grabbed his arm, "No wait man, if she knows anything about Cherry, she ain't just gonna come right out and tell us. We got to make her tell us on her own." Tommie said. "We gotta play shit smart."

Lukie nodded. "Yeah, you right!" Silence hung between the two friends momentarily before Lukie snapped his fingers. "I got it. Watch me."

Lukie strolled into the store and pretended to look at the bras. He watched Tawni as she went from table to table browsing. Again, he couldn't help noticing her big ass. Tommie was right she had the biggest ass he had ever seen. It was bigger than Pinky's, another porn star.

Tawni picked up several items and made her way to the cash register. Lukie followed behind her. After the transaction was completed, Tawni took her bags and headed out the door. Lukie saddled up next her and stopped her just as she exited the store.

"Whoa beautiful, can I help you with those bags?" He said putting on his best smile.

"No." Tawni started walking away.

Lukie ran behind her. "Don't be so hasty, beautiful. I just wanted to get to see you smile that's all." Lukie said. "Why, what did you think I wanted?"

"I'm not even going to tell you." She looked behind her at the ass she was packing and let a little smile form at the edge of her lips.

"Now that's what I'm talkin' about. But that smile has nothing on you, beautiful." He observed her body again. "Cause all of you is smiling."

Tawni blushed. "Thanks for the compliment."

Lukie seized the opportunity. "I hope you don't take this the wrong way but you look familiar to me. Have you ever been a model?" Tawni shifted the bags in her hand. She was charmed by Lukie.

"No, I'm not a model but I have been in pictures before." She replied.

"I knew you were someone famous! A face like that is made for stardom."

"Thanks again." She giggled.

"So, you an actress?"

"Yes I am and a damn good one too." She confirmed.

"What movie was your latest role in?"

"I do adult movies." Tawni said proudly.

"Oh, maybe that's why your beautiful face looks so familiar to me. Do you do private showings?" Lukie asked.

Tawni licked her lips and looked Lukie her up and down again. She thought he was too young for her to take on as a John but something about this young man intrigued her senses. "That can be arranged for a fee. I do nothing for free." She said. "I hope you understand. Even though you are a cutie."

He smiled. "Well in that case, book me. I ain't got no problem paying for a dime piece like you." Lukie lied. "So when we gonna do this?"

"You can give my agent your phone number and he'll be in touch." She said pointing to Big Blue who had been watching Tawni and Lukie the whole time. "He'll tell you everything you need to know, prices included."

"Your agent?" Lukie reared back to look at the big black man who looked like a Sumo wrestler. "You sure he not gonna try and kill me?" Lukie hesitated.

"Oh don't let the big man stop you. He's cool. He's my bodyguard. Give him your number and he'll arrange something." She saw his hesitation. "Or are you scared now little boy?" Tawni remarked.

Embarrassed by Tawni's remark, Lukie rattled off his number to Big Blue who put the number in an iPhone. When he was done, he walked away.

Tawni was about to walk out until he said, "What's your name!?"

Big Blue replied, "You won't need to know her name! But I'm sure you'll remember her face."

A week later, Big Blue rang Lukie's phone and gave Lukie specific instructions. After agreeing to the specifications of the deal, Lukie called Tommie and Aniya.

PLAN OF ACTION

"He said what?" Aniya said. She and Tommie both asked in confused unison.

Lukie put his beer down on the coffee table and repeated what he was told. "Big man said that he would pick me up and take me to meet the girl that has no name. I am not to bring any cell phones or other electronic devices such as a camera or camcorder and of course no weapons."

Aniya sprung up out of the chair and stood in front of Lukie, hands waving. "Lukie, I don't think meeting this strange woman is a good idea. You don't know where you're going and you don't know who you're really going with."

"I gotta take that chance."

"How do you know for sure that she's really an adult movie star?"

"Trust me, Aniya, she's for real. I know that big ass anywhere." Tommie chimed in.

Aniya threw Tommie shade. "I'm not laughing or smiling about that shit."

"Come on, boo, stop trippin'. You and I both watch the flicks. As a matter of fact, why don't I put one on that has her doing her best work."

Aniya rolled her eyes, as Tommie shot up the stairs and looked through his collection. He knew each DVD's content. He had them arranged by the performance that the actresses gave. It was easy to find the DVD with Tawni in it. It was in the number five slot in his DVD holder. He grabbed it, kissed the cover and ran out the bedroom back down the steps.

He placed it in the player. The movie began with several minutes of advertisements for other DVD's. Tommie skipped ahead until he got to the first scene of the movie. Carnival was the first one on the screen. It opened up with Carnival sitting poolside in a lounge chair with nothing on but a robe. She was having a drink and talking on the phone.

Lukie's surprise showed all over his face. He pointed to the TV and burst into laughter. "Man, that's a fucking midget. You shitting me right?" he said.

They continued to watch the DVD as Carnival's male co-actor appeared in the shot. He approached Carnival and they made small talk before Carnival opened up her robe to reveal her little body. She had small titties that looked like two little bumps on her chest. Carnival had a small waistline and her pussy was clean-shaven. The white male actor opened up Carnival's short stumpy legs and dove in between them tongue first.

Aniya shuddered and scrunched up her face. "Ewwwe, that's just fucking nasty." She waved at the TV. "I don't want to see that shit Tommie and I can't believe you watched that shit yourself."

Tommie ignored Aniya and pointed at Lukie whose jaw was dropped.

"Wait you ain't seen what she can really do!"

He pressed fast forward on the tape and stopped to catch Carnival's little legs wrapped around the man as he held Carnival up by her ass in mid air. Carnival humped up and down on the actor as he carried Carnival around the room. She looked like she was riding a bucking horse from the way she was throwing her hands up in the air and fucking the man's dick. Lukie was glued to the TV in fascination and Aniya was appalled. Tommie hit the fast forward button again and Tawni appeared on the screen.

"Stop, right there!" Lukie yelled.

Tommie hit the pause button and all three leaned forward, towards the TV and studied the face on the screen. Both Tommie and Lukie looked at each other.

“Yep, that’s her. Without a doubt, that’s the same woman from the mall.” Lukie said.

“Okay now that we have that established, Tommie, take that nasty shit out of my DVD player.” She rolled her eyes. “I can’t believe you actually be watching that type of shit.” Aniya continued.

Tommie took the DVD out and put it back in its jacket. “Alright, Aniya.”

“Okay, Lukie we need some type of plan. You just can’t roll up in that bitch with nothing.” Tommie said.

“Man, I don’t even know where that place is!” Lukie replied.

“Exactly, that’s why we need to brainstorm.” Aniya said.

For two hours, Lukie, Tommie and Aniya went through several plans of spying, attack and communication. All plans would be hard to execute without some type of communication. Lukie was going to have to play this out by ear. All he needed now was for big man to call him with the day and time of pick up.

ROUND 2

Stic rang the house phone and waited for an answer. He didn't give Damon time to say hello before he voiced his request. "Damon, take Cherry over to my special room and wait for me."

Damon sucked his teeth. "Okay, Stic."

"You got a fuckin' problem now, D?" Stic asked.

Damon averted the question. "We'll be waiting for you. Because as you know, the world stops when you move." He hung up the phone.

Stic looked at the phone and mumbled. "What the fuck was that?" He said to himself. "I'ma have to put that mothafucka in his place. I'ma fuck that ass so hard, he won't be able to shit for a week."

Cherry gasped when she entered the room. Just about every imaginable sexual object of pain and pleasure was there. Damon knew what the room held but was seeing for the first time the huge cage, that was now hanging in the middle of the room. This is what Stic had the workers building in secrecy.

Stic's cologne was carried through the air and entered into the room before him. Damon's dick instantly jumped and he silently scolded himself for his dick's behavior around Stic. Stic came through the door wearing a sweat suit and slippers.

He nodded to Damon and said, "I need several cameras set up around the cage, Damon. And I need you to get on top of that now."

Damon hesitated momentarily until Stic rolled up in his face.

"What the fuck is going on with you, D?"

Damon stared back at Stic. Their eyes locked in a stare. Damon was not about to let Stic punk him in front of Cherry. Damon broke the stare as he averted his eyes towards Cherry. She was wringing her hands in hope of Stic not going off right now. Damon saw her concern. He stepped away from Stic to complete his task.

Once the cameras were put in place, Stic examined them to make sure he would get the right shots. He stopped in front of the cage and adjusted the lenses on the camera. It was time for his show.

"You can leave now, D. Close the door on the way out " Stic said never looking Damon's way.

"Whatever, Stic." Damon rolled his eyes at Stic and turned on his heels. He was so not feeling Stic right now. He slammed the door as he departed.

"Fuck that, nigga!" Stic spun around to face Cherry. He seductively looked her up and down. "I need for you to get in the cage. I need to shoot a scene with you while you in it."

"I worked this morning, Stic, why can't one of the other girls shoot this scene?" Cherry asked. A quick slap to the right side of her face answered her question. She rubbed her bruised skin.

"Bitch, are you telling me that you ain't working no more today?" Stic yelled. "Are you saying you running shit now?"

"No, Stic." Cherry held the side of her face and slowly shook her head no. She loathed this man.

"Well get that ass in the damn cage then!"

Cherry stepped into the huge cage. She instantly felt like a trapped animal. She had no idea what Stic's intentions were. She watched as Stic repositioned the tripod with a camcorder attached to it. He then grabbed a bag that was sitting on the floor next to the tripod. When the camcorder was at the perfect angle he wanted, Stic entered in the cage with the bag. He slammed the door shut and locked it. The metal slamming against metal sounded like a jail cell. Cherry only heard that sound once and that was when her mother got locked up for having two small viles of crack in her possession and Cherry went to see her.

Stic took several items out of the bag and tossed it on the floor of the cage. "Turn around and face the cage."

She followed orders. In his hand was a pair of bondage handcuffs. He shackled Cherry's wrists with them and then shackled her wrists upward on the horizontal bar that ran between the vertical bars of the cage.

"Stic, what are you doing?" She asked in a soft voice.

"Shut the fuck up, bitch."

Cherry began to sweat. She wondered how long it would be before Stic took her again. She could do nothing with her wrists cuffed high above her head. She couldn't see Stic but she could hear him behind her taking off his clothes. He reappeared completely naked and in his hand was the remote to the camcorder and to Cherry's device. He pressed the remote control and the camcorder's record light turned red. He dropped the remote down by his foot and kicked it into a corner of the cage.

He pressed himself up against Cherry's ass and grinded his dick in between her ass cheeks. Stic was so turned on that he could have cum on her right then and there but he waited too long to get her pussy again. He was not about to cum that fast.

He leaned harder into her back and whispered, "Cherry Pie, relax. You're gonna like this." Stic chuckled.

He licked the back of Cherry's neck and his dick jumped to attention. Cherry recoiled. And it didn't help repel him when the smell of her *Bvlgari Jasmine Noir* perfume only enticed him further. He bit her on the collarbone and then bit her on the shoulder. Cherry tried twisting her body away from Stic's sexual foreplay but being handcuffed to the rails would not allow her the leverage she needed to deter him.

Stic thought about this scene for a long time. Today he was playing it out live. He was going to get him another slice of Cherry's pie. Stic lunged his hand between Cherry's legs and aggressively rubbed her pussy. She tried keeping her legs closed but this didn't stop Stic from roughly jabbing his fingers into her dryness.

Stic prompted Cherry's legs to spread when he whispered in her ear that he had the device. He spit in his hand and rubbed it over his throbbing dick. He pressed the tip of his dick behind Cherry, grabbed her locks and wrapped them around his hand forcing her head to be held in an upright position. He grabbed her tightly around the waist with his free hand and proceeded to push his way into her pussy. Cherry let out a painful yell.

Stic was acting like a jockey with the reins in his hands as he pulled Cherry's locs, as he gave three brut pushes before he entered her world. Cherry yelled out again in pain. Stic grabbed Cherry tightly around her waist and fucked her from the back. Cherry was mashed against the bars in agony. Her breasts and ribcage felt like they were being pushed through the small opening of the bars in the cage. Her wrists were on fire and felt like they were being ripped from her arms. Cherry's legs were beginning to feel like Jell-O.

Stic felt her legs trying to fold, so he grabbed a hold of the bars for additional support and leverage. This was just what he needed. He fucked Cherry deep and hard. He looked like a crazed dog. All Cherry could hear was his deep grunts each time he plowed himself into her.

Cherry could not move while Stic held her captive between his arms while holding onto the bars. She thought her insides were dead. She was numb and her vaginal lips were beginning to swell from Stic's abuse. Stic was on the verge of cuming. Just as he hit his peak, his finger pressed the button on Cherry's device causing her to convulse. He let out a loud yell of pleasure as Cherry's jerking and twitching on his dick caused him to cum so hard, that his legs buckled. He fell to the ground, dropping the device beside him.

Cherry's ravished body hung listlessly by her handcuffed wrists. She was semi-conscience. Stic lay on the cage floor waiting for strength to return to his legs. He found the remotes and gathered them up. He hit the stop button on the camcorder, unlocked the cage and stepped out. He put his clothes on and immediately felt the phone in his pants pocket ring. He walked away from the cage to take the call.

Damon slipped out the door unnoticed. He saw what Stic had done to Cherry. Cherry was telling the truth about Stic using some sort of implanted device on her that caused her to have seizure movements. The hate he had for him went to the next level.

Several minutes later, Stic called the house phone and Damon picked up. "I'm done doing what I needed to do. Go take care of Cherry." Then the line went dead.

Damon went back into the room and unlocked a battered Cherry from the cage and took her back to her bedroom. He laid her on the bed and examined her. Cherry's wrists were swollen and Damon could see swelling around her vaginal area. He quickly filled a tub with warm water and Epson salt for Cherry to soak in. He didn't like what was happening to her and he certainly wasn't feeling Stic's brutality of Cherry and himself. As of late, Stic was on some other shit now and Damon didn't like it and was getting too fed up.

FIELD TRIP

With what little strength she had left, Cherry pushed herself up onto the bed. She lied down and stared at the ceiling. She had enough. It was time for her to man up. She got up off the bed, turned off all the lights, closed her bedroom door and sat down in the middle of the floor. A black shroud of darkness enveloped her like a warm blanket. She welcomed the darkness with an open heart.

Cherry hadn't prayed since she was a little girl. Her Aunt Betty taught her how to pray when she would take Cherry to church with her and Aniya. At the thought of her cousin and her man Lukie, Cherry's demeanor changed. She breathed slowly in and out and let her mind drift to another time. Her thoughts were scattered at first and then she made them all line up. Cherry was in deep meditation. In her mind's eye she saw what had to be done.

"Cherry, I came to check on you, are you alright?" Damon asked appearing in her room.

He turned on the light and was startled to find Cherry sitting in the middle of the floor in a trance like state. Cherry hadn't heard him come in. She didn't even realize that the lights were on and Damon was standing over her calling her name.

He reached down and gently nudged Cherry's shoulder breaking her out of her abstraction. Wild eyes looked up at Damon. He abruptly took a step away from her as she stood up. He watched her walk over to her dresser and stare at herself in the mirror. An eerie silence surrounded the room.

Cherry turned around and faced him. "Damon when you go into town, I want to go with you."

"Chile, you know I can't do that." He paused. "You know Stic ain't gonna let me take you outta of these four walls. He would kill us both."

"Damon, look at me. Do you see what Stic has done to me? Did you know that he took me in that room and raped me again?"

Damon sighed hard and looked into Cherry's dark eyes. "I saw what he did to you, Cherry. I never left the room." Silence filled the room again.

Cherry reached for Damon's hand. "Damon, I know you couldn't help me without getting yourself into some shit with Stic. But if you ever wanted to help me now is the time. Stic took me away from my home and my life. All I want to do is ride to my house. Can you at least drive me by my house? I'm begging you, Damon, please." Cherry cried.

She broke down and bawled uncontrollably. Damon pulled Cherry into his chest and patted her on her back. After an hour of pleading and coaxing and crying some more, Damon agreed to sneak Cherry out of the Compound.

"Okay, I'll take you later this week. Just stop crying."

He held her in his arms as Cherry cries subsided. He hated what Stic was doing to her and he really wanted to help her in anyway he could. After Damon left her room Cherry closed her door and let out a hideous laugh. She had Damon fall for her act, hook, line and sinker.

"Come on, chile, you know we gotta get out of here before they return from work." When she seemed to be moving slower he got serious. "Come on now! Damon whispered.

Everyone was down at the studio filming another movie. Luckily, Cherry didn't have a part in the movie that day. Damon ushered her down the steps and into the massive garage. They got in the one of the three Escalades and drove off.

Cherry was laying low in the backseat of the truck. The windows, as all of the windows for each vehicle that Stic owned, were tinted black. No one could see her anyway. They made small talk but Cherry wanted Damon to shut the fuck up. She really didn't feel like saying shit. Her mind was reeling with seeing her house for the first time in weeks. She wanted to take the truck and run to Aniya's house, but that would put Aniya's life in danger. She loved her cousin too much to do that.

Follow the plan. Just follow the plan. When Damon made the left turn down her street, Cherry's heartbeat quickened. The Escalade seemed to hesitate going any further and it slowly crept up to the projects apartment building.

"Stop right here." Cherry said pointing to apartment complex D.

Damon watched Cherry with intensity as she stared straight ahead at the building. As usual the projects were full of activity. Low totem pole drug dealers stood in the front of the buildings. Loud music blared from someone's open window. Scattered debris was thrown about the front and sides of the buildings. The alleys were a haven for junk. Old car parts, washing machines, bags of clothes and bags of trash, lined the alleys like decorative planters.

Hot young girls, barely fourteen, were out scandously clothed, showing way too much ass and too much titty. They all had at least five bags of cheap plastic hair weaved on their heads. Some of them looked like a bag of skittles exploded on their heads. Every color in the damn rainbow could be found there.

Rouge boys whose pants sagged so much, if they had to run for cover, they wouldn't make it because their pants would surely be the death of them. And all of them looked like they had not bathed in weeks. Everyone and everything was at its usual in the hood. Nothing changed at all. Cherry turned away from the scene.

She surprised Damon when she said, "I'm going up to see my mother I'll be right back, D."

"Oh hell naw! Are you goddamn crazy? Girl, you ain't getting out of this damn truck." Damon screeched trying to snatch Cherry by the arm.

But he was too late. Cherry was out the door and down on the sidewalk. He didn't know what to do. Should he go after Cherry or wait? He couldn't leave Stic's truck out there like that and besides; he didn't know which way Cherry went. Then he looked at himself. He was dressed in drag today. If he got his ass out that Escalade and went anywhere near the projects, he might not make it out alive.

"Fuck, Fuck!" he screamed. He hit the center of the steering wheel with his fist. "I'ma kill that bitch when she gets back."

Cherry made her way up the steps to her building without being seen and if she was, no one acknowledged her. She walked down the pissy smelling corridor to her door. She stood in front of it and stared at the numbers. Apartment D-24.

She took a deep breath and put her hand on the knob and slowly turned it. It was unlocked. Her mother must be expecting Drug Company. She walked in the faintly lit living room. She shook her head in disgust as nothing had changed. She heard footsteps and her body tensed.

"Frog, is that you. I've been waiting," she saw her daughter's face instead, "oh my God, Cherry! What are you doing here?" Bonita asked.

Cherry cocked her head to the side as if the question was stupid.

Bonita caught the look. "I mean, I didn't expect you. Where have you been? Oh Cherry, I'm glad to see you. Come here, baby." Bonita walked over with one and a half arms outstretched to hug her only child. Secretly Bonita was pissed that Cherry just showed up at home and was now getting in the way of Frog coming over to get her high.

Cherry put her hand up in a stopping fashion. "Don't touch me."

Bonita stood where she was. Her jones was kicking in and she didn't have time to talk to Cherry at the moment. Still, she smiled at her child. "Cherry, I've missed you, baby. You know I love you right?"

Cherry didn't utter a single word as she watched her mother fidget from one foot to the other. Bonita kept looking at the door behind Cherry. *Yep, she is expecting someone to bring her some drugs,* Cherry thought.

Bonita tried another approach. "Cherry, I didn't want anything to happen to you. And it hasn't. Look, you're here, alive and well."

"Really? Are you fucking serious? You have no idea what has happened do you? Or do you even care? Did you care about your own sister who was murdered because of you?" She paused. "The same night Aunt Betty was murdered was the same night Stic came and got me. It was on my birthday. And I bet you haven't even bothered to look for me. You didn't give a rat's ass 'cause you were too busy getting high. " Cherry shrilled.

"I am not in the mood to talk about this right now, Cherry. And quite frankly, I'm not sure why you're here." She looked at her hands. "You ain't got no bags with you, so it don't look like you're moving back in."

"You are the worst mother on earth."

"So you came back here just to tell me shit that I already know? Well you listen here, Cherry, I'm still your mother and you will respect me. I ain't apologizing no more for what the fuck happened. I couldn't stop it from happening. But I did save our lives whether you liked the way I did it or not."

"Your actions ruined my life!"

"Do you see my hand? Them mothefuckers came in here looking for your ass and when I didn't tell them, they put my hand in the garbage disposal. I lost my arm because of you, Cherry." Bonita seethed.

"Did you just say you lost your arm because of me? Tell me you didn't just blame me for your arm, ma! What they should have done was stuffed all of you in the disposal. That's where you belong." Cherry hissed back.

Bonita lunged at her daughter. They came together like two dancers stepping on each other's toes. Cherry grabbed her mother's dirty T-shirt and held it tightly. She got in her mother's face and said, "I love you, mother but I hate and despise you and what you have done to my life."

Bonita's wide eyes stared back into Cherry's. She draped her good arm over Cherry's shoulder and looked lovingly into her only child's eyes. Cherry condemned her mother.

"This is for Aunt Betty, Aniya, Lukie and me. I wish you well on your fucking journey!" Cherry sucked her teeth and continued on, "You're ass ain't going to heaven. I hope you go straight to hell. I got a feeling that Stic will be joining your ass soon."

Bonita fell to the floor in a crumpled heap. Cherry stooped down, kissed her mother on the cheek and closed her eyelids as she removed the butcher knife from deep within her chest. She methodically walked up the steps to the bathroom, rinsed off the knife and wrapped it in a towel. She made her way to her old bedroom and put on another shirt and pair of pants. She put the towel and her bloodied clothes in a bag. She went back down the stairs.

Her eyes scanned the room one more time and then she saw it. She raced over to the étagère' and snatched the picture off it. She threw it in the bag. Not once did she look at her mother as she locked and quietly closed the door. She slipped down the stairs and into the dark of the alley.

Damon was livid. He knew he shouldn't have trusted Cherry. How was he going to explain defying Stic's rules? So when Cherry knocked on the passenger side door, scaring Damon so much that he screamed and ducked down in the driver's seat of the truck, he had thoughts of murder on his mind.

"Damon, let me in its, Cherry." he popped the locks on the truck and Cherry slid in the back seat.

"Oh my God! Girl, I just about died! I didn't know if you were coming back. Girl, I didn't know what to do. You know I want to whoop your ass. You got my nerves on edge, chile. Damon exclaimed.

"I wasn't going to do you like that. I know that Stic would kill you and kill me too. Ain't no sense in both of us dying out here."

"Whew, you ain't never lied about that!" Damon said fanning himself.

Cherry whispered to herself, *I came to do what I had to do anyway. It's all good now*. Damon never noticed Cherry's change of clothes or the bag that she had on the floor at her feet. All he wanted to do was sneak Cherry back to the compound undetected as soon as possible.

THE PICK UP

A black cargo van pulled up in front of Lukie's house. He was expecting it. He peeked out the window trying to get the license plate number to text to Tommie but the license plate was covered with a distortion cover. He couldn't make out any of the numbers. All he could text was that the vehicle was black and that it was a cargo van. He answered the phone call and told Big Blue he was on his way out. He snatched his house keys off the table and was out the door. He opened the van door and slid in the seat.

"What's up, man?" Lukie said.

"Nothing, get out so I can search you." Big Blue replied never looking over at Lukie.

"It's good, man. I did what you said. I ain't got no cell phone, camera or gun." Lukie said.

"That may be all well and good, but I need to see for myself. Now get out."

After the search was done and it revealed that Lukie had nothing, they got back in the van and drove off. Lukie suddenly wasn't feeling this shit and he most certainly was not happy about not having his piece or cell phone on him. Several minutes into the ride, the van pulled over to the side of the road.

"Yo, man, what we stopping for?" Lukie questioned.

"Shut the fuck up!"

Big Blue handed Lukie a black hood. "Put this on before we go any further!"

Lukie looked at the hood and shook his head no. "Man, I ain't puttin' that shit on. What I need to put that on for?"

"Because where I'm taking you is a location that is not public knowledge. Either you put it on or I can drop your ass off right here. It makes me no damn difference. You're the one that wants to spend time with the lady. It's your call, dawg!"

"Man this some crazy shit. You didn't tell me this was part of the visit." Lukie said. "Ya'll acting like I'm about to be murdered or something."

Big Blue awaited Lukie's decision. "Whatcha gonna do, dawg? I ain't got all day to be fucking with you." Big Blue said.

"Man, how I know your ass ain't crazy or some shit and trying to kill a nigga." Lukie said. "How I know that's not part of the plan?"

"Because you would be dead already! I ain't gotta take you know where to do it." He paused. "Now I'ma ask you one more time whatcha gonna do?"

"I don't know about this shit!" Reluctantly Lukie put the hood over his head and Big Blue secured it with the locking drawstring.

Tawni promenaded into the room in a pair of six-inch glass heels, a pair of leather chaps and a leather bra that was cut away to reveal her heavy breasts. In her hand was a cattail whip that she was smacking in the palm of her hand. Lukie tensed up.

Tawni laughed. "You ain't scared is you?" she mocked, as she stood wide legged in front of Lukie. "I ain't gonna hurt you that bad."

"I ain't scared." He replied. "I'm just not into certain things that's all."

"Good. Let's see what you got!" Tawni straddled Lukie in the chair and rubbed his head between her breasts. She reached down and grabbed Lukie's crotch roughly. "I see you have a little something here."

"Damn, don't be so mean. Let's ease into this." He wasn't feeling the situation at all. "First, what's your name? Can we at least start there?"

"You can call me anything you want." Tawni said. "I'll be anything or anybody you want me to be."

"No name huh?" He said. "You serious about not placing a name to that pretty face?"

"There's no reason for you to know my name, boo. I'm not your girlfriend or wifey and I ain't tryin' to be. I'm here to do what you're paying me to do. Have a little fun and put a smile on that face."

"Fair enough! You got anything to drink then?" Lukie asked. "I need something to warm up."

"I got a lot of bottles behind me." Tawni said nodding her head towards the dresser where several bottles of liquor adorned it. "You can take whatever you want."

"Why don't you fix me something then?" He said.

Tawni slid off of Lukie's lap and headed towards the bottles. She chose a bottle of Hennessey and poured a healthy drink into a glass.

"You got any coke to go with that." Lukie asked. "I don't take mine that way."

Tawni opened up the mini fridge and retrieved a coke. She popped the top and poured some into the glass of Hennessey. She seductively sauntered back over to Lukie with drink in hand. He slipped it from her hands and marveled at the statuesque woman before him.

"Where's yours?" he asked. "I don't like to drink alone."

"I don't drink on the job." Tawni replied. "You're off of work, not me."

"Come on, pour yourself a lil' something and toast with me." Lukie urged. "It won't hurt anything and it sure will help me have a nice time.

Tawni poured a shot of vodka in a glass and threw it back with no problem. "Better now? Because I'm ready to get down to business."

"I bet you can't do it again." Lukie challenged.

Tawni sighed, poured a double shot this time and downed it in one breath. The vodka left a hot burning trail as it slid down her throat. Instantly Tawni felt woozy. She could handle a mixed drink or two but today she was showing off and it was catching up to her.

"You look good with a buzz." He said.

"Let's do what you came to do." She said to Lukie while she made smacking sounds with her mouth. "You should be warmed up now."

Lukie downed his drink and sat the glass on the nightstand. He stood up and grabbed Tawni by the waist and turned her around. He gawked at her phat ass. It was so big and round that Lukie was captivated by it for a moment and fell to his knees, rubbing his face on her ass cheeks. He forgot all about his girl.

His dick sprang forward in his pants. Tawni made each of her ass cheeks pop in Lukie's face. She turned around and the front of her leather thong greeted Lukie. She forcefully pulled his head toward her snatch and grinded herself against his face. Lukie quickly stood up and pushed Tawni against the wall and held her hands above her head. He wanted to take control of the situation.

"Ummm." Tawni purred. "I like a man that likes to be in charge."

"Then your gonna love me." Lukie said.

He grinded his dick in between Tawni's legs and kissed the side of her neck making her legs weak. Tawni's head was beginning to spin from the alcohol she consumed minutes earlier. She was feeling the effects of it when Lukie challenged Tawni to another drink. She declined but he egged her on, calling her a punk. She fell for his challenge. She released herself from his grip and brought back two glasses. One was vodka and the other was Hennessey.

Tawni hoisted the glass up to her face. "Okay, baby boy. Here's to you. Let's drink!" Now she was feeling too good. With one too many shots under her belt, Tawni was stretched out on the bed and Lukie was lying on top of her. She was completely drunk. This was a perfect time for Lukie to question her.

"You ever had a threesome with another woman?" Lukie pried.

Tawni laughed at Lukie's question. "I'm an adult movie star. Duh. " She giggled. "You answer the question."

"I sure would love to have a threesome with another girl. Do you think any of your other adult movie stars would have one with me and you? That's a fantasy of mine I always wanted fulfilled."

"Me and you?" She laughed. "I ain't said nothing about having a threesome with you. We ain't even had a twosome yet. Slow your roll."

"Come on, Shawty. I like's you and I really want a threesome with you and someone else." Lukie said kissing Tawni on the neck again causing her to shudder under him. "I just want to know if you can make that happen or not. The answer is yes or no."

Tawni slurred, "Okay, babbby, if that's what you want. Umm, maybe next ti…time. Okay?"

"I'm talkin' 'bout now!" Lukie said, "I already have a girl in mind that I saw on a DVD my boy had. You was in that joint too. That's how I knew it was you."

"Oh yeah? You saw me and sh…shit? Did you…you like it?" Tawni asked? She couldn't really form her sentences like she wanted to. "T-that would explain why you wanted to hook up with me. You like what you saw."

"Yeah, girl, I saw you. You was working that pussy out." He smiled at her. "You and that other girl!

"Shiiiiiit, I be doin' the thang in my movies!" Tawni bragged. "They come from miles a way to hit this pussy."

"So, you gonna hook me up with you and the girl that was in the movie with you?" Lukie asked. "I'm trying to have a good time tonight. With both of you."

Tawni thought for a minute about who Lukie could be referring to. She only worked with three other girls and they all were actresses from another crew.

"Do you know which girl it was in the movie? Whats's her name?" Tawni asked.

"I'm not really sure. I think its Cherry." Lukie said trying to keep his heart rate from excelling.

Tawni thought for a minute and then a wide smile stretched across her face. Bingo… He waited and then Tawni spoke. "I know of a Cherry. But we ain't never did no movies together. She do her own movies with other girls. But if you want her and me I think I can arrange for her to come through." she frowned. "Shit, me and Cherry don't really get along but when it come to that green we can put our differences aside."

Lukie was about to burst. This was the news he had been waiting to hear. He quickly asked, "Is she some place where you can call her?"

"Yes."

"So pick up the phone. Let's do this!" he said.

Tawni tried to sit up but her head was beginning to swim. She gathered her thoughts and replied, "It ain't gonna be today 'cause I think she left her room with Stic to do a movie tonight. I'm not sure where she is now."

Cautiously Lukie said, "She left her room? Oh so she lives up in here with you?" He tried to act like his heart wasn't pounding out of his shirt.

"Umh hum." Tawni replied. "She's usually here."

Lukie teased Tawni some more by grinding his dick on her pussy. "So this cat Stic, is he like her agent?"

Tawni immediately knew she fucked up by letting Stic's name escape her mouth and especially to a John. She pushed Lukie off of her and stood up so quickly that she swayed and had to catch the side of the dresser for support.

"Listen, I've been babbling. Why don't we just get into the action that you came to get and forget about that threesome?" She said trying to undo Lukie's belt. "I'm tired of talking. It's time to fuck."

He thought quickly. "You got a bathroom."

Tawni pointed to the bathroom in her room. "You can use that one."

"I can't use that one. I need to light it up and I don't want to be in there shitting while you out here listening. Ain't there another one in this place?"

"There's one down the hall but you really ain't supposed to be out there unless you're leaving." Tawni said.

Lukie nuzzled up to Tawni. "Just let me go handle my business and when I get back, I'ma put this big dick up in that pussy like you want."

Tawni licked her lips. She wanted to be fucked by the young boy and she was going to make him eat her pussy until she came at least twice. "Okay, go do you and when you get back, be ready to eat this cootchie." She said fingering herself.

Tawni opened the door and pointed to a bathroom down the hall. Lukie closed the bathroom door behind him and waited for a minute before he opened it back up and peeked out. He didn't see anyone so he slid out the door and down the hall. The place was larger than he thought. There were several doors that were wide open but no one occupied the rooms. He carefully made his way to a staircase and eased down the stairs careful not to make a sound. He stopped midway and looked to his left and right. It was hard to see from that point so he crept down several more stairs. He heard voices coming from the left side and quickly ran down the remaining stairs and hid behind a wall. His heart was beating a hundred miles a minute. The voices were coming closer. He leaned as far back into the wall as he could get and held his breath.

Big Blue came down the hall to check on Tawni and her John. He tapped on the door and waited. When Tawni didn't holla through the door that everything was good, he opened it with his key. Tawni was passed out on the bed and the John was not in the room. Big Blue started his search.

Lukie stepped out of the depths of the wall to look around for something that would give a clue as to where he was. He swiftly moved several more feet and stopped. His eyes scanned the room. If he found a phone, he could call Tommie and the number would appear on Tommie's cell phone. There was no phone.

Lukie softly treaded back out the room and tiptoed down another hallway. His eyes fell upon an office. He snuck in and immediately went over to the desk. He carefully shoved around some papers looking for an address when his eyes fell upon the phone. He eased the receiver off the cradle and was stopped when there were no buttons on it. *What the fuck?* He thought.

Bewildered, he looked at the receiver in his hand and then back to the cradle on which the receiver laid. He couldn't believe there was no way to dial out. He put the receiver to his ear and listened to the phone ringing. A voice answered. Lukie put his hand over the receiver and listened. He wanted to ask who the person was but he thought better of it. He carefully put the receiver back on the cradle. He needed to get back to Tawni's room. He was sure she was looking for him.

Lukie crept back out the office and headed back, when he was snatched from behind by his shirt and punched in the face. With his lights out, Lukie was dragged back towards the stairs.

Cherry and Dominitra were on their way to the kitchen when Big Blue passed them dragging an unconscious Lukie. Dominitra stopped Big Blue. "Who is that?" Dominitra asked.

"A John that got away." Big Blue retorted. "He was too busy roaming the house."

Dominitra shook his head. "Whose John was it?" he asked.

"Tawni's, but she got drunk and passed the fuck out and this motherfucker right here decided he wanted to be nosey and shit." Big Blue said. "This why we gotta keep our eyes on mothafuckas the entire time."

"Maybe he was looking for a way out. You did say Tawni was passed out drunk."

"Fuck that. Tawni knows the rules. She wasn't even supposed to be drinking. You know as well as I do that the liquor is for the Johns. Now I got to take his ass down to the basement." Big Blue said.

Dominitra shrugged his shoulders and moved away from Big Blue. When he did, Cherry let out a loud scream and put her hands up to her face. Both Big Blue and Dominitra froze.

"What's wrong with you, girl? You look like you seen a ghost. You know this motherfucka or something?" Big Blue questioned.

"No, I just thought he looked like someone I knew but he's not." Cherry quickly lied.

Big Blue's eyes constricted. "You sure about that?" He questioned again. "Because the look in your eyes tell me otherwise."

"Yes…I'm sure. He's not who I thought he was."

"Good, cause if you know this nigga that wouldn't be a good look. You know I would have to tell Stic."

Cherry lowered her head and turned away from Lukie. "I said I don't know him. I'm not sure what else you want me to say."

Big Blue gave Cherry and Dominitra a look before he continued dragging Lukie towards the basement. After he left, Dominitra grabbed Cherry by the arms. "Come with me." He pulled her in the office. He pierced her eyes with his. "You know him don't you?"

Cherry couldn't catch her breath. She felt like she was about to pass out. Her mind was all over the place. How did Lukie find her? He was here. He was actually in the compound. Her Lukie was there and she had to find a way to get him and her out of the Compound alive.

Dominitra shook Cherry again. "Girl, I'ma ask you one more time, and you better not lie. Who was that boy?"

"That's my boyfriend!" Cherry wailed. "And I love him!"

Dominitra gasped. "Goddamn it, Cherry what the fuck is he doing here?"

"I don't know, Dominitra." She shook her head. "I don't even know how he knew I was here. We haven't spoken since I was kidnapped by Stic," Cherry replied.

"Did you call him the day I snuck you out of here? Because if you did that's gonna get me in a world of trouble."

"No, I had another issue that I resolved that day."

"What are you talking about, Cherry?" Dominitra asked.

"It's nothing, Dominitra. But I didn't call my boyfriend."

"Damn, Cherry when Stic finds out Tawni let a John loose in the house, he's gonna hit the fucking roof! I got to be honest, chile, Tawni or your boyfriend might not live through the night. But I know you know that."

Cherry put her fingers to her mouth and shushed Dominitra. "I ain't trying to hear that, Dominitra." Cherry replied. "I don't give a shit about Tawni but we need to get to Lukie out of here. If he's here it's because he was trying to save me."

"Cherry, you know we can't get near that boy. The minute Big Blue calls Stic it's a wrap. All we can do now is pray for your boyfriend. And Cherry, you know you can't say a word or even act like you know him, right?"

Cherry didn't respond she just grabbed Dominitra's arm as tears slid down her cheeks. "I don't want him to die. Please, I don't want him to die."

Dominitra wiped the tears away. "I can't make no promises on that. Come on, girl, we need to visit Tawni's ass and find out what the fuck she knows. And if the answers ain't right, it won't be Stic her nasty ass got to worry about. Trust!"

It had been hours since Tommie or Aniya heard from Lukie. Aniya paced the floor, wringing her hands. "Are you sure you don't know where he went?" She repeatedly asked Tommie. "Because I don't know about this situation."

"Damn it, Aniya, stop asking me that I told you a hundred times, I don't know where Lukie went. All he texted me was the color of a cargo van. And that ain't saying shit right now."

"Tommie, I got a bad feeling that some shit happened that wasn't supposed to happen. What the fuck are we gonna do?"

PRAYED UP

"Tawni, wake the fuck up!" She didn't move. "Get up, tramp!" Dominitra hollered. He slapped Tawni's face several times. "Your ass shouldn't have been drinking anyway! You were supposed to be handling business!"

Tawni slowly opened her eyes. "What's this all about?"

Dominitra wasted no time in grilling her. "Tawni, you're in a fucking mess! Wake your dumb ass up and listen to me!"

"Okay, okay." She rubbed her head. "I'm up! Just don't hit me no more!"

"You know that John that you brought in here?"

"Yes."

"Well he's in the basement waiting for Stic to come and probably kill him."

Tawni shook the cobwebs from her head and rose halfway and sat up on her elbows. "What? What's going on?" She asked. "Why would he be there?"

"You done fucked up now!" Dominitra said. "You know damn well that you aren't allowed to be drinking with no John in here. Big Blue caught him downstairs sneaking around! And you know what that means!"

Cherry interrupted Dominitra, "Where did you meet him, Tawni?" Cherry inquired. "Why are you with him! It doesn't make any sense."

Tawni sat up straight to address Cherry. "He's a fucking John. What difference does it make where I met him? He don't mean sh…"

Cherry stopped the rest of the words from tumbling from Tawni's mouth when she reached around Dominitra and grabbed her throat. Tawni's eyes bulged out of her head from the pressure that was being applied from the chokehold that Cherry was giving her.

Dominitra clutched Cherry's hands and removed them from around Tawni's throat. Tawni sprang up off the bed and charged at Cherry. Dominitra stepped in causing Tawni to run into him. He pushed Tawni back on the bed with his left hand and pinned her down. He got in her face. "Listen up, bitch, if Stic comes in here trying to beat everybody down for this shit, I'ma snap your scrawny neck back. Do you hear me? This is all your damn fault. He should've never been allowed to leave the room."

Cherry was impatient. She interrupted, "Tawni, I'ma ask you again, where did you meet that man and how did he get here?"

"Say something, because you may have put all of our lives on the line." Dominitra responded.

Tawni knew Dominitra was right. When Stic heard about her fucking up she was going to be dealt with. She was scared. "Let me up, Dominitra!"

Dominitra released his hold on Tawni. She scrambled to the top of the bed and sniveled as she told Cherry and Dominitra about Lukie approaching her in the mall and how she set a date with Lukie through Big Blue, like she does any other John. "I'm so sorry about this shit, Dominitra."

Cherry paced the room. "Shit, shit, shit!" she yelled to Tawni.

"What the hell is your problem? Your ass ain't in the sling mine is!" she said to Cherry.

Dominitra cut in, "No, bitch, all of our asses are in a sling. You better think about what you're gonna do when Stic gets here." Dominitra grabbed Cherry by the arm and pulled her to the door.

Tawni stopped Dominitra. "Dominitra, you got to help me." Dominitra reared back and looked at Tawni like she was crazy. "He's going to kill me if you don't say something."

"Help you? The only help I can give you is to tell you to pray, bitch. You need to pray for yourself and what's left of your life!" He pushed Cherry out the door leaving a scared Tawni to her thoughts.

INTEL

Tommie touched the button on his phone to end the call. Aniya could hardly wait for him to get off. "So?" she asked anxiously.

"Well nobody knows much about the DVD's or where they come from. I asked Blick to look into some shit for me. He's got some connections so maybe he can come up with some information that we can use." Tommie said.

"What about the car? I know damn well motherfucka's know whose car that is?" Aniya said. "Somebody had to have seen it."

"Yeah, I asked about the magnum and Blick said several people drive a car like the one I described. He's lookin' in to that now, Aniya. All we can do is wait for some type of lead."

"Well why can't we get out there and start asking around ourselves, Tommie? We should have been doing that all along. I need to find my cousin right now!"

Tommie gently put his hands on Aniya's shoulders. "You know we just can't be out there in them streets asking about people. First of all we don't know who the fuck we're asking about and second, we don't know who the fuck we're dealing with. And Aniya, I ain't trying to go through losing you behind this shit. We done lost too much already. Just wait for Blick and the rest of my crew to come back with something. I know they will."

Aniya put her head on Tommie's shoulder and cried. He held her with all his might. For the first time, Tommie felt a twinge of fear creep through him. He had a bad feeling too that shit just wasn't gonna come back right for Lukie or Cherry. He pulled Aniya closer to him and rocked her in his arms.

A COMPOUND BEAT DOWN

"Uhm umm…Blue, are you telling me some John done ran up through my shit?" Stic paused as he waited for his response. He was talking to Blue on the phone. "I know you not telling me this shit. You were supposed to be looking out for things."

"I'm just as shocked as you."

"Whose John was it?" He waited for a reply. "I need to know who's gonna answer to this shit."

"Tawni's. She got drunk and let him out of her sight. He was all through the house snooping and shit."

"She did what?" He yelled. "So is the John sitting in the Truth?"

"He's still there."

"Good." Stic continued. "I don't need to tell you to keep both of them bitches on lock down right? I'm out of town and should be back in a day or two. I will deal with them then." Stic tapped the phone to end the call.

He scrolled down his listing until he came to a name that he was looking for. He tapped the button to place the call. He told the doctor to be at his house in two days. He tapped his phone to end that call and sat back in the seat of his first class flight.

Tawni was going to need a doctor when he got down whooping her ass. If the John lived, he would never want another piece of pussy either. And where the hell was Damon? Stic thought as he looked out the plane window and made another mental note.

He was going to have to show everyone at the Compound that he meant business.

MAYHEM

Cherry and Damon were in his room behind closed doors. "Okay, we got two days before Stic returns." Damon said. "After that, all hell will break loose."

She looked scared. "How do you know that?" Cherry asked, face still wet with tears.

"Because I saw Big Blue call Stic on the private line. I picked up the phone in the office and listened in."

"I want to see Lukie!" Cherry said grabbing him. "Take me to him, Damon. I want to see him before they kill him."

"Chile, Big Blue got that boy on lockdown. You ain't gonna be able to get anywhere near him." She looked upset. "Do you think that your boyfriend came to find you?" Damon asked. He was not in drag now.

"I don't know, Damon. I do know that Lukie wouldn't have propositioned Tawni for sex in a million years. Lukie must know something. He must've found out I was here some kind of way."

Their conversation was cut short by screams from downstairs. Damon and Cherry raced down the steps to find Trailer Trash, Carnival and Tawni yelling at one another. The minute Damon appeared, they bombarded him with their grief.

Trailer Trash yelled the loudest to get her point across. "Tawni just told us what happened. I can't believe that she let this shit go down. You know Stic is going to go loco when he gets here."

"You telling me something I already know." Damon said.

"She has put us all in jeopardy. I don't want to be involved in her shit but you know Stic ain't going to let it go down like that." Trailer Trash complained. "I want to kill her."

Carnival slid her two cents in, "Yeah, Damon, I ain't going down for her either. And where the hell was you? Aren't you supposed to be watching over everything in here? How did you let this happen?"

Damon's temper rose. "Everyone shut the fuck up! Ya'll need to throw that shit back on Tawni's doorstep. Not mine. I didn't even know her ass had a damn John in here. I'm not your shadows! I do have business of my own and it don't includes watching ya'll every five minutes."

Trailer Trash threw her hands to both sides of her head and screamed at the top of her lungs, "I can't take this no more! I got to get out of here now!"

Carnival screamed back at Trailer Trash, "Then why don't you just go kill yourself! That would be one less life that Stic's crazy ass will have to take."

Trailer Trash ran off screaming down the hall.

Carnival addressed Tawni. "If Stic comes in here with his guns a blazing and puts his hands on me because of you, I will kill you in your sleep!" Carnival pushed Tawni out the way so she could get by.

Tawni ran back to her room. Cherry and Damon looked at one another despairingly. Shit was about to hit the fan.

Lukie regained consciousness and was desperately trying to free himself, to no avail. He was securely bound to a chair. His head was covered with the same hoodie that he was given, come to the Compound. It added to his sense of trouble. There was nothing Lukie could do but wait for what lie ahead.

THE PLAN

Cherry and Dominitra devised a plan to see Lukie. Cherry put on her lowest pair of hip hugger jeans and a wife beater. The jeans sat low on her hips and made her ass looked like Beyonce's in them. The wife beater was torn in the middle and Cherry's firm breasts came bursting through. She went in search of her bait. It didn't take her long to find him.

Big Blue was sitting on a chair reading the paper when she appeared. "Hey, Blue." she said seductively. Big Blue put the paper down in his lap and acknowledged Cherry. She was standing in front of him, legs apart. He grinned so hard, his face hurt. "What you doing?"

"What's up, Cherry?" he asked. "I ain't doing too much of nothing."

"I'm bored so I came out to see what was going on with you." Cherry fluttered her eyelashes at Big Blue. "I hope I'm not interrupting you."

He let his eyes freely roam across up and down Cherry's body. He especially lingered at her lips. Ever since Cherry came to the compound, he wanted her on her knees in front of him with her lips wrapped around his dick bobbing her head back and forth. "You could never bother me and I know you know that."

Cherry happened to lick her lips and Big Blue's muscle between his legs came to life. He hid his hardness behind the paper. Cherry leaned over to give Big Blue a better look at her breasts. He had seen all of the other girls butt naked, but he had not had a chance to view Cherry in all her glory. His dick jumped again straining to be let lose. Cherry sensed she had an opportunity.

She ran her hand up Big Blue's leg and slowly eased it towards his dick. When Cherry's hand rested on his manhood, Big Blue almost burst a nut. Cherry moved in for the kill. "Blue, you know I've always wanted a big Teddy bear like you. Somebody who could make me feel safe and warm."

His eyes widened. "Really? I never knew that."

"Because I never told you, Blue. Don't you see the way I be lookin' at you sometimes." She lied. "I can't keep my eyes off you. God only knows what I'd do to you with the rest of my body." Big Blue's grin told Cherry all she needed to know.

She snatched the newspaper from his hands and pushed him back into the chair. Big Blue pulled Cherry down on his lap. He pulled her head to his and stuck his tongue out. He sloppily tried to French kiss Cherry and she wanted to gag. Blue Blue didn't know how to kiss and his salvia was all over her mouth.

Damon peeked around the corner to see Cherry working her plan. Now he could slip down the steps and see Lukie in the basement and tell him that Cherry was there. The rest of the house was quiet because everyone else was in their rooms, waiting on pins and needles for Stic's arrival. Damon was at the basement door. He slipped the key in the and lock and turned the handle. Suddenly, he stopped.

"Oh shit!" Damon said. He closed the door and ran down the hall. "Stic is here!" he said out of breath. "I can't believe he is here!"

"Oh my God Stic is here?" Cherry screeched while on Big Blue. "Why is he so early?"

Big Blue bolted up from the chair, pushing Cherry down to the floor. He was gone like a bolt of lightening. "Get the fuck out of my way!"

Cherry threw her hands up in the air, "I thought you said he wouldn't be back for two days, Damon!" she yelled. "I thought we had more time."

"I know, I know, but that motherfucka must have turned around and came right back here. I was real with you about what I heard on the phone. God only knows what will happen now."

Cherry felt faint. All she could think about was what would happen to Lukie. The horrible part was Lukie didn't even know Cherry was there.

Stic, Moop, Damon and Big Blue were in the basement. Big Blue just snatched the hood off of Lukie's head. Lukie adjusted his eyes to the light. Stic cracked his knuckles as he walked around the chair. He stopped in the back of the chair and asked Lukie from behind, "Why are you in my house? And before you answer the question, know that I'm not in the mood to hear no bullshit."

"I was invited by that nigga right there!" Lukie said nodding his head at Big Blue. "I didn't sneak in here any other way."

"I see." He nodded. "So you were here because you were with one of my bitches. Is that right?"

"Yeah, man. I came to see that big ass bitch." Lukie said.

"Big ass bitches are everywhere in my house."

"The one with the huge ass!"

"Tawni… awe yeah she does have a big ass." He smiled. "It makes men do stupid shit like come up in another nigga's place looking for shit. If you think I believe that, you can also believe I'ma let you out of here unscathed." He paused. "What were you looking for in my house, man?" Stic said walking back around to the front of the chair.

"All I needed was a phone, man. I was just looking for a phone. I needed to call my boy!" Lukie replied. "Something came up. That's all."

"Now I know that Big Blue over there told you the rules right?"

"Yeah, man, he told me. But I had an emergency and since ya'll don't let a nigga have a cell phone in here, I needed to find a phone."

Stic threw a right punch to Lukie's face. "Nigga, you think you just gonna roll up in here and defy my rules. You must be crazy!" Stic yelled and threw another punch to Lukie's face. "Rules are in place for a reason! Yet you decided to break them!"

Blood spewed from Lukie's nose and mouth. He was disoriented from the blows. Stic was tired and mad as hell. He had cut his trip short so he could come back and handle the business at hand. He was pissed because his business deal was put on hold by this little nigga sitting in front of him. No one fucked with his money. Partially luckily for Lukie, he didn't feel like playing the torture game today. He had too many other asses in the house to whoop. So he wanted to kill the noise in front of him now.

He leaned down in Lukie's face. "I don't like motherfucker's who don't play by the rules. If I didn't know any better I'd think you came up in here to rob a motherfucker. Is that what you was down in my office doing, looking for shit to steal?"

"You got me all wrong, man!"

"I'm never wrong. A little wanna be thug nigga like you would do some shit like that to a man of stature such as myself. If I let you." He pointed at him. "You can't get your own so you wanna come take mine. Fuck that shit! Don't nobody take anything that belongs to me."

Lukie tried to tell Stic he wasn't there to rob him but the air in Lukie's stomach left him winded after Stic threw a heavy punch in its place. Lukie doubled over in pain. "I wasn't trying to rob you." He said as pain crept up the front of his body.

Stic turned to Damon. "The next time a slip up like this happens and your punk ass is here, this is what the fuck I'ma do to you!" He turned to Moop, "Take that little nigga out!" Moop raised his gun and pointed.

"Lukie!!!" Cherry screamed. "Please don't do this to him! This is all a misunderstanding! He doesn't deserve to die."

Everyone snapped their heads as Cherry came running in the room. Lukie raised his head in astonishment as Cherry ran towards him. She was here. He found Cherry. "Cherry!" Lukie yelled back. Before Cherry reached the chair, Lukie's head snapped back as Moop shot him between the eyes. Cherry fell down at Lukie's feet screaming his name.

Stic stood over top of her. He reached down and grabbed her by her locs. Damon wanted to help Cherry but he knew Stic wouldn't hesitate to have him shot just like he gave the order to shoot Lukie. Stic tightened his grip around Cherry's hair.

"I told you I would kill your boyfriend! But you thought I didn't recognize him. I'm not stupid, little girl. You are." he said. He snatched his hand out of Cherry's hair. "Take her back upstairs," he said to Big Blue. "Tell Batman to get his ass over here and cleanup now!" he yelled to Moop.

FED UP

Damon watched a heartbroken Cherry being marched back to her room by Big Blue. He understood her heartache. He was feeling the same thing now for Stic. He loved Stic but he finally realized that no matter what he did, Stic would never be his man or love him the way that Damon deserved to be loved. And right now Stic didn't love any of his bitches up in the Compound either.

He could hear Tawni's yells and screams down the hall. He headed toward her room and stood outside and listened. Damon could hear Tawni's cries of pain as Stic unmercifully beat her. Stic snatched the door open of her room, just as Damon slid into a hall closet door. Stic didn't see him.

But several minutes later, the house phone rang. Damon knew there was going to be some drama when he picked it up. Sure enough, he was summoned to Stic's office. Stic stared Damon into the eyes, "I'm going to ask you one time, D, did you know that was Cherry's boyfriend? Before you answer understand that I'm not in the mood for no bullshit."

Damon played his part. "Chile, I didn't know anything about him period. No one knew besides Big Blue that Tawni even had a John in the house. This was all his doing not mine or the other girls." He paused when it looked like he didn't believe him. "Stic, none of us knew that believe me, honey."

Stic crossed the room to where Damon was standing and bitch slapped him. "If I find out your faggoty bitch ass is lying you know I will kill you right?"

"I know, Stic." He grabbed his face.

"Good! You let Carnival and Trailer Trash know that I'll be back for them. I haven't forgotten about them. No stone or ass will be left unturned." Damon held the side of his face as he watched Stic leave the office.

When the door closed, he waited a minute before opening the office door again. When he did, he watched Stic and Big Blue leaving out the house together. Damon had to be quick about his search. He found what he was looking for and quickly put it in his pocket. He went to Cherry's room and found her on the bed still crying over Lukie.

Damon sat on the bed next to her and whispered, "Cherry, take this and make one phone call to your cousin. Give her this address. You have to talk fast because Stic can track this phone and there aren't but five minutes left on it."

Cherry willingly snatched the phone from Damon's hand. "Damon, where did you get this?"

"From Stic's office. It was an old phone he used to make some deals with. I wasn't sure if it was still in the safe but it was." He replied. "So I'm giving it to you to use. But like I said, you have to make it quick."

"How am I going to get out of here?" Cherry asked. "I don't know what to do. I'm confused."

"Don't you worry about that! A bitch gonna handle some shit like a grown ass man. You just tell your cousin to be at this address. Now get dressed, make the call and wait for me to come and get you." Damon said.

Cherry hugged Damon and started dialing numbers.

KNOTS FOR LOOSE ENDS

Aniya turned over in her bed and reached for her phone that was ringing. Her head was throbbing from all of the excitement but she reluctantly answered. "Hello."

A voice screamed into the phone. "Aniya.... Aniya! I need you help! Are you awake?"

Aniya gripped the phone harder and pressed it closer to her ear. "Cherry? Is that you? Am I actually talking to my favorite cousin?"

"Yes!"

"Oh my God where are you, girl? Talk to me, Cherry!"

"Aniya, listen, I need you to come to this address and get me. Don't ask any more questions. This phone is about to die. Now take this address down! Now!"

Dominitra had everything he needed in the Gucci purse that he slung over his shoulder. He made his way to Tawni's room. She was in the bed suffering from the wounds and bruises that Stic inflicted on her. She winced in pain as she lifted her head to see who was coming in her room. When she saw it was Dominitra she relaxed.

Dominitra stood over Tawni as she sputtered out an audible sentence. "Dominitra, what's wrong with you? Why are you in here? To beat me too?"

Dominitra sighed heavily and sat down on the edge of Tawni's bed. Tawni eyed Dominitra suspiciously. Dominitra said, "You got an innocent young man killed today, Tawni. Did you know who he was?" Tawni didn't answer. "That boy was Cherry's boyfriend. He came to rescue his damsel in distress and instead, he hooked up with your evil ass and now he's dead."

Tawni's mouth fell open. "Cherry's boyfriend? So that's why he asked for Cherry. That slick ass motherfucka! He came up in here pretending to want me and all he wanted was Cherry's ass." Tawni whenced in pain again. "I knew that bitch was nothing but trouble the minute Stic brought her here. But he wouldn't listen to me. Now I got my ass whipped for nothing. I should beat her ass too!"

"You don't even care about what happened do you?" He asked, shaking his head.

"It ain't my fault that nigga dead. I told his ass to use the bathroom in here. But he wanted to play Ace Detective and shit. If you asked me, he got exactly what he deserved. And Cherry needs to be sent right behind him."

Dominitra fingered the clutch on her Gucci. She turned to Tawni. "It is your fault, hoe. You set him up to be your John."

"I can't help who my Johns are. I don't do background investigations prior to fucking them. That motherfucka rolled up in my space talkin' 'bout he wanted to get with me. Did you tell Cherry her boyfriend caused Stic to go fuckin' crazy in here? I know I've got several ribs broke."

"This ain't nobody but yours, cunt!"

"And why the fuck are you standing there defending that bitch anyway? You need to be calling the doctor over here so he can fix my shit! Fuck Cherry and her boyfriend. He ain't have no business here in the first place. Stic needs to be in there stomping a mud hole in Cherry's ass, not mine!" she yelled. "Fuck Cherry, do you hear me? Fuck her!"

"Tawni, I dislike you something fierce." Dominitra said. "And it's been a long time since I could truly say that about a person and mean it."

"I don't li…"

Dominitra leaned down and with one quick motion, came across Tawni's neck. Tawni's instantly grabbed at her neck with both hands and brought them to her face. Thick red blood covered her hands like red velvet gloves. She tried to scream but the gurgling sound of her chocking on her own blood was the only sound she could make and the last sounds Dominitra heard, as he gently closed the door and walked out.

Aniya put her clothes on faster than the speed of sound. She grabbed her phone and her keys and was out the door like a shot. She put the address in her GPS system and sped out the garage, ensuring that the garage door came down. On the way, she phoned Tommie and told him to meet her at the address Cherry provided.

Dominitra made his way to Trailer Trash's room. He hadn't heard a peep out of her for a minute. Her door was locked when he tried it. He took out his master key and unlocked the door. He did a quick survey of the bed and Trailer Trash wasn't in it. He saw the bathroom door was closed. He quickened his steps and opened the door and smiled when he saw Trailer Trash. She was swinging from the iron clothes rod that ran from one end of the bathroom to the other.

Dominitra remembered when she complained to him that she needed a triple supported bar anchored in her bathroom, so she could hang up some of her heavy wet clothes. Now there she was with a thinly torn sheet wrapped around her neck swinging lifelessly back and forth. Dominitra's job there was done by Trailer Trash's own hand. He slipped out of her room. He was on his way to his next victim when Carnival appeared out of nowhere scaring him. He willed his heart to slow down. He had to play it cool.

Carnival stopped and pointed to Dominitra's purse. "Hey, Dominitra, you stepping out girl?"

"Yes. I am. As a matter of fact, I need to ask your opinion on something. I got it right here in my purse." Dominitra opened up his purse and took out a plastic bag with a long strip of duct tape attached to it. He showed it to Carnival. "What you think about this girl?"

"It's a plastic bag, Dominitra. Is that like some new fashion statement or something?" Carnival asked.

"Yes it is, Carnival. I need to see how it fits." he answered as he moved closer.

"Fits on…"

Carnivals words were caught in the bag as it was slipped over her head and Dominitra wrestled her to the ground. He held Carnival between his legs and arms in a death grip and quickly and tightly wrapped the duct tape around her neck. Carnival fought with all her might but she was no match for his strong hold. The bag sunk in each time Carnival took in a breath. Dominitra watched as the midget took her last breath and died in his grip. He picked her up and carried her to Trailer Trash's room and put her in the closet. He closed Trailer's door and locked it. "Three down. Two to go." He said to himself.

RESCUE ME

"Where are you?" Tommie asked his girlfriend on the phone.

"I'm on my way to get my cousin. I can't believe I actually got a hold of her. If I wait any longer, she may die."

"Well I'm almost there, Aniya. So pull over and wait for me. I don't want you going there alone. You don't know what kind of shit might be waiting for you! This entire thing is dangerous."

"No, Tommie. I can't. Cherry needs me and I'm going to get her. Now! You just hurry your ass up and get there yourself!" Aniya hollered. "We might need backup."

She clicked her phone shut and listened to the GPS's verbal commands. She was less than five miles away. She couldn't wait to see her too. She needed to make sure she was okay. Cherry didn't say anything about Lukie. Was Lukie there with her? Maybe Lukie didn't find Cherry. It didn't matter, within a few minutes Aniya and her cousin would be reunited and she would find out all she needed to know.

Stic was at the main house with Big Blue discussing the next animal act for Trailer Trash. This time, Stic wanted Trailer Trash and Carnival in the movie together. He had it all set for both of them to be fucked by a Great Dane. "Find a saddle for the Great Dane. I want Carnival to ride that bitch like a damn horse and then I want that motherfucker to fuck her midget ass like a man!"

"I got the dog and I'm sure I can find some type of saddle for Carnival, but how you gonna get her to let the dog fuck her?

You know she gonna trip out!" Big Blue said. "That was never her thing. It's Trailer's"

"Come on, Big B, you shouldn't even have let that shit come out your mouth, man. You know them bitches gonna do whatever the fuck I tell 'em to do. So if I say fuck a dog, she will fuck two!" Movement in the room caused Big Blue and Stic to look up. Stic furrowed his brow. "What the hell are you doing up here I didn't call you?!" he barked at Damon.

"I have something to show you that I found on one of the girls. You both need to see this." Dominitra reached inside his bag and pulled out his gun and let off several rounds. Before Big Blue could reach for his shit, he hit the floor dead. Stic was draped over a chair. Dominitra put the gun back in his purse and ran as fast as he could.

Cherry was antsy. She kept looking out the window and then back at her door. Any minute now, she expected Stic to run up in there and kill her and the rest of the house for such a daring escape. She was relieved when Dominitra came rushing through the door instead.

"Come on! We gotta hurry up, Chile!" Dominitra said out of breath.

Cherry didn't need to be told twice. She and Dominitra ran down the steps and out the door. Dominitra had the Escalade pulled in front of the Compound. They jumped in it and headed to the main road. Cherry was holding onto the door handle as Dominitra drove the Escalade on two wheels like it was on fire.

"Dom?" Cherry softly said.

He averted his eyes towards her and said, "It's best if you don't know anything, Cherry. Keep your eyes open for your cousin."

Several minutes later, Dominitra was out of the thickness of the wooded Compound's area and on one of the main roads. Cherry's eyes were peeled open for her Aniya's car. Dominitra drove slowly enough so Cherry could look. Cherry sat up on the edge of the truck seat. She began to sweat. Was that her? Was that Aniya? "Dominitra! Stop! That's her right there." She pointed. "Flash your lights!" she hollered.

Dominitra flashed his lights. Two cars were waiting off to the side of the road. Cherry stretched her neck to get a better look. "That's Aniya and Tommie," Cherry excitedly exclaimed. Cherry jumped out and ran over to Aniya's car.

Aniya could not believe her eyes. It was her cousin. It was Cherry. She flung open the door and ran towards her. Tommie followed behind Aniya. Aniya and Cherry embraced hard. With tears running down both their cheeks they hugged and kissed one another. Tommie joined them.

Dominitra pulled up to the elated bunch. "Cherry, I've got to get out of here. The police will probably be hovering around soon. If you must tell them anything about me make me look good." Dominitra smiled.

"I have nothing to tell the police about you, Dominitra!" Cherry ran over and hugged Dominitra. They lingered a moment. "I do know this, you saved my life. Not sure why you did it, but I'm happy you did."

"It was time."

"Do I even have to ask?" Cherry said. "About what happened?"

Dominitra put his hand over Cherry's. "No, Cherry. You don't want to ask. I'll be long gone when you do anyway. Listen, Cherry, you are special to me and I love you. Now, you get your ass outta here and take your cousin with you, 'cause I don't know what demons Stic may have unleashed upon his death. You know that motherfucka wanted to still run shit beyond the grave. Who knows if he'll get his wish?"

Dominitra pressed his foot down on the accelerator, squealing the back tires and sped off into the darkness of night. Cherry jumped back in Aniya's car and they sped off as well with Tommie following behind them.

Tommie called Aniya's cell phone and told her to put it on speaker. He wanted to hear what happened and if Cherry saw

Lukie. Cherry started her story from the beginning of the rape to her capture. She didn't tell Aniya about her killing her own mother. She would wait and tell her that without Tommie listening in.

It wasn't Tommie's business and as much as she loved him, he wasn't family. Tommie cut in. "Cherry...Lukie went to find you. Did you know that?"

"Yes, I saw him." She replied. She sounded sad.

"Oh my God, then where is he Cherry?" Is he still out at that place?" Aniya asked.

Cherry stopped talking. Aniya cast her eyes towards her cousin. She saw the pain in her eyes. A blood-curdling scream and then another and another left Cherry's throat. Tommie threw his cell phone on the passenger side of the car. He could hardly see because of the tears that flowed from his eyes. He didn't have to ask Cherry to know that Lukie was dead. But Aniya did.

"Is he dead?"

"Yes! I can't believe he is gone!" Cherry screamed at the top of her voice and broke down into heavy sobs.

Aniya moved the car over into the far right lane, so she could slow down and let her mind process what she just heard. "Tommie, are you still there?" Aniya softly asked.

"Yeah, I'm here." Tommie sniffed.

Tommie and Aniya were in disbelief. This shit wasn't happening. It just could not be true. No one would have ever believed this shit, unless they were actual witnesses like Aniya, Tommie and Cherry had become.

CLEANUP CREW

Skibop and Batman were on their way over to do the clean up of Lukie's body. But they weren't in any hurry so they stopped at, *Corinthian's Lounge* and had a of couple drinks. It wasn't like they weren't cleaning up the dead almost every week. There was no urgency.

"Man, there's some ugly ass bitches up in here tonight." Batman said looking around the lounge. He banged his hand on the bar and a short older woman took his order of Jack and Coke and a bottle of Corona. He tapped Skibop on the shoulder and pointed his finger at the waitress. They immediately fell into a fit of laughter. "That one has to be the ugliest."

Skibop finally stopped laughing long enough to say, "Man, that bitch's legs are so bowed, you could put an arrow in between them and shoot that motherfucka out on Lord Baltimore." They laughed again and gave each other some dap.

Batman said, "Man, she got Ricketts!" Skibop looked at Batman like he had two heads. "Oh, I see you don't know what the fuck I'm talkin' 'bout. They call that shit Ricketts nigga. My grandma told me that shit comes from malnutrition!" Skibop continued.

Batman studied the woman's deformed shaped legs and said, "Well that bitch must have made up for those missed meals, 'cause a bitches stomach is wrapped around her back!"

They burst into laughter again. Skibop finished his shot and downed his beer. Batman ordered another Corona. Skibop's phone rang. He lifted his phone out of the clip that was attached to his waist and answered it. Immediately he was annoyed.

"Man, have ya'll left to go over to the Pound and clean up? I ain't feelin' Stic blowing up my phone eleven hundred times about this." Moop hollered into the receiver.

"Nigga, chill. We on the way, shit!" Skibop said. He tapped Batman on the shoulder. "Let's bounce."

Aniya tapped Cherry on the shoulder. "Cherry, wake up, boo. We 'bout ready to get off 695. I called and reserved us a hotel room out in Woodlawn. So we can get some rest."

Cherry opened her eyes. She had a migraine headache and her body was sore and tired. She yawned and stretched. "Thank you, cousin."

Tommie called Aniya's cell phone. "I'll be over to the hotel soon. I need a minute though."

He was still dealing with the sudden knowledge of Lukie's death. He needed to pull over to get his self together. He never dreamed that he would be without Lukie. They had been best friends since grade school. Now his nigga was gone.

Tommie wept briefly and then suddenly stopped. He opened his phone and placed a call to Blick. When Blick answered he gave Blick the run down of events that transpired. Tommie had to be sure if Lukie was really dead. He also wanted to know any, and all details of the others that Cherry said were out at the Compound. Lastly, he wanted Blick to find out whom everyone was that Cherry named in her story. If anyone was left alive, Tommie was going to kill them himself.

SEESAW

Batman and Skibop were smoking a blunt. The music was several decimals louder than any human ear should have been able to listen to. Skibop was driving and weaving on the road. The effects of the alcohol were starting to kick in combined with the blunt he just smoked. He was feeling good.

"Damn, nigga, can you drive and shit?!" Batman screamed over the music. "You making me thin you 'bout to kill us. Slow the fuck down."

"Yeah, I got this! Just make yourself useful and roll another blunt!" Skibop yelled back. They burst into a high laughter. Skibop's phone rang again. "Shit, I bet that ain't no fucking body but that damn Moop calling me again!" He reached in his pocket and pulled out his phone. He went to flip it open with his thumb. When he fumbled it, the phone dropped in between the seat and the driving console.

"Shit!" He yelled. He tried to stick his fingers down in between the seat but couldn't reach it. The car swayed as Skibop's phone continued to ring. "Shit, I need to get my damn phone!" he yelled again.

Skibop took his eyes off the road to search for the phone. The car veered off into the oncoming lane. Before Skibop could regain control of the car, it smashed into another car on the opposite side of the highway. The impact sent Skibop and Batman's car flying into a tailspin where it stopped at the edge of an embankment and teetered.

Aniya and Cherry's car was slammed head on and crashed into a utility pole causing the pole to snap in half and fall on the roof smashing it down onto the girls.

Batman and Skibop were woozy. When the wooziness cleared, they both looked at one another with anguished faces. Skibop looked out his window. He could see nothing below his door. He felt the bowels of his stomach churning. His heart rate shot up and he couldn't get his breathing regulated. He looked over at an equally scared Batman.

"Don't move, Batman." Skibop whispered. "You can kill us if you do. Be real careful."

"I fuckin' ain't doing shit!" Batman whispered back. They felt the car sway back and forth in a seesaw motion. Batman was so scared he burst out crying. "I don't want to die man. Not this way! I wanna live. Shit! There's so many things left I want to do."

"Man, shut the fuck up with all that bitch ass crying and shit! We need to see if we can get out of here before this shit slides off the edge." He observed with his eyes without making a move. "Look around, without moving, for a way to get us the fuck out!" Skibop yelled. "That's what you need to be doing."

"I'm not going to be able to do shit unless I move!"

"Well be careful!" Skibop yelled.

Batman tried the door but it wouldn't open. He looked over at Skibop. "Shit nigga, what we gonna do? If we move while we're in the front seat of this car, it's going to tip over! We can't win for lose right now."

"Shhhh. Let me think!" Skibop said. He slowly turned his head to get a better view of the backseat. Maybe he could climb in the back and open the door and roll out before the car fell. He started to move when the car dipped down in the front.

"Ohhhh, Shit!" Batman hollered. "Nigga, keep your ass still before we be over the fuckin' edge!" He said holding his chest. Batman thought he was going to have a heart attack from the fear alone. "Whatever you doing ain't working! So stop!"

"This doesn't look good." Skibop added.

"Nigga, all we can do is be still and wait for a motherfucka to see us." Batman said. He wasn't a praying man and didn't know the first thing about a prayer, but he bowed his head and began to pray that night.

Tommie was done mourning for the moment. He needed to get to the hotel so he and the girls could get a good night sleep, before they headed out tomorrow morning. He wasn't sure where they were going but he knew Cherry had to leave town as quickly as possible. And if Cherry left, Aniya was leaving with her and he was going where ever Aniya went. Tommie drove back in traffic and was preparing to turn off onto his exit when he did a double take. He slowed his car as he came up on the accident. "That looks like Aniya's car!" he said out loud.

Tommie threw his car in park, opened his driver side door and practically fell out. He found his footing and immediately ran over to Aniya's car. He screamed her name as he ran to the car but got no answer. He raced around to the driver's side and saw Aniya and Cherry wedged under the weight of the utility pole and the hood of the car. He heard other voices in the distance. He turned towards the voices and saw Batman and Skibop's car on the edge of the embankment. He ran over to them. Skibop and Batman were grateful to see him.

"Help us, man!" Skibop hollered through the window. Tommie looked at the car on the edge and then back at Aniya and Cherry. "Don't let us die, man! Please!" He reached out his hand for Tommie's.

"Did you hit them?" Tommie asked with a frown.

"It was an accident, man. We didn't mean to hit that car! Come on, man help us get out of here!" Skibop pleaded. "We got families who love us. We don't want to go out like this."

Tommie took another look at Aniya and Cherry. When Tommie didn't see movement within Aniya's car, he ran around to the back of Skibop and Batman's car and gave it one hefty push. Skibop and Batman's screams sounded like they were on a roller coaster, as the car slid over the edge and dropped several hundred feet down. It nose dived straight into the ground instantly crushing Skibop and Batman to a liquefied pulp.

LAID TO REST

Tommie made sure Aniya and Cherry had the best money could buy for the funeral. He chose two identical lace dresses. Aniya had the white dress and Cherry had a pink one. Both looked like angels as they laid in their pink inlaid coffins. There was not a dry eye at the double funeral. Mourners came in to pay their last respects to the cousins who loved each other so much, they gave their lives.

Just two days earlier, Tommie attended Lukie's funeral. Tommie and Blick were sitting on the back pew of the church when Blick tapped Tommie's arm. Tommie's eyes followed a woman who was dressed in a large black hat and black Channel suit. When she walked by, *Flower Bomb* perfume filled the space she had previously occupied. She bent down and kissed Cherry on the cheek. All eyes were on her as she sashayed up to the casket. She looked at Aniya and then at Cherry. She gently rubbed Cherry's face followed by a gentle kiss on both cheeks.

"I'm going to miss you, sweet Cherry." Dominitra said. He wiped his eyes of the sorrowful tears and walked out of the funeral home. Dominitra strolled to his car and got in. He was due to catch a plane. He had wired some money that he stole from Stic's safe, to an account in France. Dominitra always wanted to go to Paris and today he was getting his wish. But he was not going to leave until he saw Cherry one final time to say goodbye.

Dominitra strapped himself in the seatbelt and put the key in the ignition. Volts of electricity shot through his body. Dominitra wouldn't stop convulsing. When his body came to an abrupt hold, Dominitra looked out his window. He mouthed the words, "Fuck you," before he fell over dead onto the steering wheel.

Stic rolled up the window of his car and pulled away. He patted his chest and smiled as he felt the bulletproof vest that he always wore. He wasn't dead. He fooled them both.

Tommie and Blick stayed two or three car lengths behind the Magnum. Tommie inspected his gun for the hundredth time. Blick was driving. He had his gun tucked in between his legs. They followed the magnum as it slithered its way through traffic like a snake.

"Blick, my man, do not let that motherfucka outta your sight. I don't care what the fuck happens, don't let that nigga get away!" Tommie said.

"That bitch is as good as dead. I ain't about to lose him. But you gonna miss the funeral man."

"I said my goodbyes to Aniya and Cherry. Aniya knew I loved her and I know in my heart Aniya would want me to handle this business right here, than to be up in some church waiting for a preacher to say shit about her that he didn't even know about. So let's go!"

Stic was on the phone talking to Aston. "Look, Aston, we need to excel our production. We ain't making the supply to fit the demand. You know I don't like having people waiting on my shit. Why's it taking you longer to produce? What the fuck is up?"

Aston tried to explain to Stic that several of the formula's ingredients couldn't be bought in Maryland. He was going to have to go to New York or Chicago to get them. Stic wasn't listening. Instead, he cut Aston off.

"What the fuck you mean, you can't get the ingredients? Come on, Aston. I know damn well that can't be the reason my shit ain't being produced."

Aston continued to explain that the ingredients were the reason for the hold up and the ingredients were now harder to get. Stic was so busy yelling on the phone that he almost ran the red light. He slammed on his brakes and continued his inquisition with Aston. Blick and Tommie saw the car stopped at the light.

"Roll up on that nigga's right side. I'ma jump out to the left." Blick pulled his car up to Stic's at the light. Tommie jumped out of his car and went around the back of the Magnum and crept up on Stic's passenger side. Stic didn't notice Blick's car or the activity that had taken place. He was still screaming at Aston.

"What the fuck am I paying your white ass for? Listen here, motherfucker, you're costing me money, Aston. Either you get the ingredients by tomorrow, or they're gonna find you and your crew floating in the fuckin' Chesapeake Bay! Now do what the fuck you gotta do to make this shit happen!" He said. "And another thing…Wait, hold the the fuck on, Aston." He saw Blick at his car. "Let me see what this motherfucka wants." Stic pulled the phone down from his ear and rolled down the window. Blick was standing outside of it. "Yo, what the fuck, nigga?" Stic asked.

"Man, I need some help." Blick replied. "Sorry to bother you."

Blick scanned the car quickly and didn't see any protection in his immediate view. All he saw was the phone that Stic had in his right hand. His left hand was on the steering wheel. Blick softly tapped twice on the hood of Stic's car. Stic caught Blick looking around. He immediately knew something was up and he needed to reach for his shit without Blick knowing.

In the meantime, Stic posed the question, "What the fuck kinda help you need?"

"Some answers, nigga!" Blick retorted. Stic went to reach for his Glock when Blick raised his to Stic's head. "Easy, motherfucka. Throw that shit out here." Stic refused. Blick let a round off into Stic's dashboard. Reluctantly Stic threw his Glock out the window. Blick kicked it under the car. "Now roll down the window on the passenger side of this bitch."

"What?" Stic asked.

"Motherfucka, you heard me the first time, roll down the passenger window, nigga!"

Stic rolled down the window and Tommie immediately raised up from the squatting position he was in. He raised his nine and aimed it at Stic. "This is for my boy, Lukie!" Tommie pulled the trigger and a bullet hit Stic in the stomach. "This is for my girl, Aniya!" Tommie squeezed the trigger again hitting Stic in the chest. Blick didn't see any blood.

"Yo, Tommie, this nigga tefloned up!"

Tommie raised his gun again, "This is for my girl, Cherry. She's gonna love this one!" A single shot from a hollow point nine, pierced Stic's skull splattering it everywhere in the front of the car. Another voice resonated in the car. Tommie snatched up Stic's cell phone.

"Stic, man, what's going on?" Aston asked.

Tommie answered, "He's going to hell, that's what's going on!" Tommie closed the phone, threw the phone on the ground and killed it with two bullets. Tommie and Blick returned to their vehicle and sped away.

Aston drove down to his sister's to spend the weekend with her and her children. He was sitting at the computer when she walked in to the den.

"Aston, I know you didn't drive all the way down here to work. Now come on you promised me and the girls that we would take a trip down to the beach. So get off the computer and let's go. The girls are so excited to have their uncle Aston here." She beamed.

"I'm coming. I just have to make some changes to this document." He replied. Aston pulled up a file on his flash drive. His finger hovered above the mouse and within a few seconds, the virus he unleashed deleted the files on the flash and the hard drive. Aston then maximized the page that he currently had been viewing.

He turned to his sister and asked, "If you could go anywhere in the world, where would you go?"

His sister thought for a moment and said, "Everywhere. I would go everywhere, Aston, but you know I don't have money to travel like that so it's just a dream. Now come on, the girls and I are waiting."

"Aubrey, come here, I want to show you something first." Aston said pushing his sister towards the computer. He pointed his finger, "Look."

Aubrey glanced at the screen and then leaned further down to get a better look. She put her hand over her mouth. "Aston! What is that?"

"It's our ticket to everything and everywhere in the world."

"Is that all yours?" Aubrey asked.

"Yes it is. It's all mine. Now, go and get the girls, I'll be out in a sec."

Aubrey went to get her two daughters. Aston returned his attention back to the screen. He clicked open his bank account and then clicked open Stic's offshore hidden account in the Cayman Islands. He made the transfer and hit send.

Several minutes later, Aston was a multi-millionaire. He opened up the virus and deleted all of Stic's information. When it was done demolishing everything that he encrypted it to do, Aston pulled the flash drive out of the hard drive. He headed towards the front door when he made a u-turn and ran to the bathroom. He dropped the flash drive into the toilet and flushed it. Aston watched it swirl around and then go down the bowl. He laughed a hearty laugh and muttered to himself, "Stupid, faggot ass nigger! Who's floating in the Bay now?"

The Cartel Collection
Established in January 2008
We're growing stronger by the month!!!
www.thecartelpublications.com

Cartel Publications Order Form
Inmates ONLY get novels for $10.00 per book!

Titles		***Fee***
Shyt List	________	$15.00
Shyt List 2	________	$15.00
Pitbulls In A Skirt	________	$15.00
Pitbulls In A Skirt 2	________	$15.00
Pitbulls In A Skirt 3	________	$15.00
Victoria's Secret	________	$15.00
Poison	________	$15.00
Poison 2	________	$15.00
Hell Razor Honeys	________	$15.00
Hell Razor Honeys 2	________	$15.00
A Hustler's Son 2	________	$15.00
Black And Ugly As Ever	________	$15.00
Year of The Crack Mom	________	$15.00
The Face That Launched a Thousand Bullets	________	$15.00
The Unusual Suspects	________	$15.00
Miss Wayne & The Queens of DC	________	$15.00
Year of The Crack Mom	________	$15.00
Familia Divided	________	$15.00
Shyt List III	________	$15.00
Raunchy	________	$15.00
Raunchy 2	________	$15.00
Reversed	________	$15.00
Quita's Dayscare Center	________	$15.00
Shyt List V	________	$15.00
Deadheads	________	$15.00

Please add $4.00 per book for shipping and handling.
The Cartel Publications * P.O. Box 486 * Owings Mills * MD * 21117

Name: ________________________________

Address: ________________________________

City/State: ________________________________

Contact # & Email: ________________________________

Please allow 5-7 business days for delivery. The Cartel is not responsible for prison orders rejected.

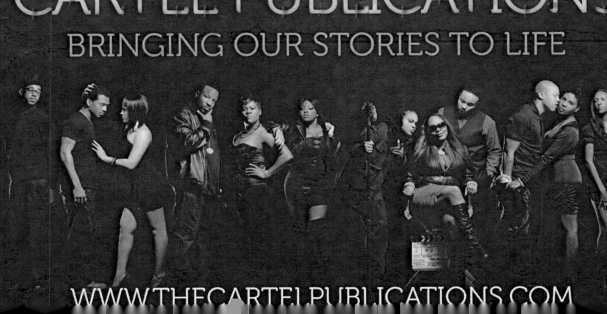

CPSIA information can be obtained at www.ICGtesting.com
Printed in the USA
LVOW041545161112

307679LV00002B/15/P